ST. THOMAS PUBLIC LIBRARY
36278008464703

D0899457

NOBODY
FROM
SOMEWHERE

JUN -- 2022

ALSO BY DIETRICH KALTEIS

Ride the Lightning
The Deadbeat Club
Triggerfish
House of Blazes
Zero Avenue
Poughkeepsie Shuffle
Call Down the Thunder
Cradle of the Deep
Under an Outlaw Moon

JUN - - 2022

NOBODY

FROM

SOMEWHERE

A CRIME NOVEL

DIETRICH

KALTEIS

ST. THOMAS PUBLIC LIBRARY

Copyright © Dietrich Kalteis, 2022

Published by ECW Press
665 Gerrard Street East
Toronto, Ontario, Canada M4M 1Y2
416-694-3348 / info@ecwpress.com

All rights reserved. No part of this publication may be reproduced, stored in a retrieval system, or transmitted in any form by any process — electronic, mechanical, photocopying, recording, or otherwise — without the prior written permission of the copyright owners and ECW Press. The scanning, uploading, and distribution of this book via the internet or via any other means without the permission of the publisher is illegal and punishable by law. Please purchase only authorized electronic editions, and do not participate in or encourage electronic piracy of copyrighted materials. Your support of the author's rights is appreciated.

Cover design: Michel Vrana
Author photo: Andrea Kalteis

LIBRARY AND ARCHIVES CANADA CATALOGUING IN PUBLICATION

Title: Nobody from somewhere : a crime novel / Dietrich Kalteis.

Names: Kalteis, Dietrich, 1954- author.

Identifiers: Canadiana (print) 20220131252 | Canadiana (ebook) 20220131260

ISBN 978-1-77041-611-6 (softcover)
ISBN 978-1-77305-910-5 (ePub)
ISBN 978-1-77305-911-2 (PDF)
ISBN 978-1-77305-912-9 (Kindle)

Classification: LCC PS8621.A474 N63 2022 | DDC C813/.6—dc23

This book is funded in part by the Government of Canada. *Ce livre est financé en partie par le gouvernement du Canada.* We acknowledge the support of the Canada Council for the Arts. *Nous remercions le Conseil des arts du Canada de son soutien.* We acknowledge the support of the Ontario Arts Council (OAC), an agency of the Government of Ontario, which last year funded 1,965 individual artists and 1,152 organizations in 197 communities across Ontario for a total of $51.9 million. We also acknowledge the support of the Government of Ontario through Ontario Creates.

PRINTED AND BOUND IN CANADA   PRINTING: MARQUIS   5 4 3 2 1

To Andie
always

... *Fitch*

He lay on the bed in back of his aging Winnebago, Fitch Henry Haut calling it the Happy Camper. Nothing happy about it these days. Not since Annie had passed.

Now having to deal with her angry side, giving him a hard time about the blood he'd been coughing up — doing it from the afterlife.

"Just means we'll be together, babe, sooner than later."

"Don't be such a boob, Fitch." The woman not taking his crap, never did in life, and not going to in death either.

"God, I miss you . . ."

"Make the appointment, Fitch."

"It's a little blood. It'll pass."

"I mean it, Fitch."

Lying in the dark, folding his arms across his chest, he suppressed another cough, waiting for the iodine taste of blood to leave his throat.

"Knock it off," she told him.

He stared straight up, fighting her with silence.

"Fine, be like a child. But I tell you, Fitch, you keep it up, this dense energy, then I won't be coming back."

"You can't threaten me, not in my own dream." Fitch sure that it wasn't the way dreams worked.

"You have no idea. Listen, mister . . ." What she called him anytime her anger peaked. "Get out of your head and feel me with your heart. First thing in the morning, you're making that call. I mean it, Fitch." Promising if he didn't, she'd stop showing up from the other side. "Put up with your stubborn nature for forty-three years. Don't have to put up with it anymore."

"What's that mean?"

But she was gone.

Fitch sitting up. Even in a dream, his own dream, the woman got the upper hand. And he coughed more blood, wiped his hand across his mouth, feeling the wet.

. . . *Wren*

The Snows set Wren up on the Murphy bed in the main-floor den. Donna Snow wanted her feeling less like a foster kid, more like a family member. Kevin Snow making it plain he just wanted to feel her.

Pulled down, the Murphy bed left a foot and a half between the desk and a shelf of books, mostly self-help books: the power of this, the art of that. Growing rich and awakening giants. Titles like *Unfu*k Yourself* and *The Subtle Art of Not Giving a F*ck*, with lots of asterisks. A grocery-store print above the pull-out, a still life with fruit and purplish shadows.

Next to the kitchen, Wren could hear the hum and rattle of the old Frigidaire, keeping her company those first nights when sleep dodged her. Propped against the pillow in the dark, she was thinking about her mom, praying for her. Wary of Kevin Snow from the start, something not right in the way he looked at her.

The third night, she opened her door, listened for sounds from the upstairs bedrooms, decided everyone was asleep and tiptoed in the dark past the noisy fridge, crossing the cold tiles, heading to the powder room in her undies, needing to pee. Kevin was sitting in the dark at the kitchen nook, a short drink in front of him. She froze.

Clicking on the light, he smiled, eyes sweeping up her bare legs. Wren covering up and hurrying to the bathroom, saying, "Sorry."

"You got nothing to be sorry about, shortcake." Kevin leaving the light on, waiting until she hurried back to her room, the hand towel held in front. Wren shutting the door hard enough, hoping to get Donna's attention. Could hear Kevin chuckling in the kitchen.

Pulling the chair from the desk, trying to prop it under the doorknob, the way it was done in some movie she'd seen. The chairback too short to reach the knob. Glancing around the dark room for something like a weapon, she grabbed one of the self-help books.

Finishing his drink, Kevin came to her door and tapped his knuckles, whispering from the other side, "Nighty night, now."

Sitting on the bed, thinking if he came through that door, she'd hit him, hard as she could, with the corner of *Unfu*k Yourself*.

Hearing the stairs creaking as he went back to his room. Wren seeing under the door, waiting until he switched off the hall light. Knowing he'd be back.

. . . the Vancouver model

"So one minute she lays it on me, lets me know she's eating for two. Eyes me to see how I'm taking the news. Next thing I'm getting slapped." Cooder Baio took the safari hat off, set it down and shook his head, his mouth twisting up. "Right in the Taco Bell."

"You took a pregnant girl to Taco Bell?" Angel James Silva swung his arm over the seat back, the grin sending his lazy eye into a squint — one eye looking at him, the other looking for him, the way Cooder saw it.

"Said she felt like Mexican. Plus, hey, did I know she was preggo?"

"Man, you hear yourself?"

"What?"

"Can't talk like that, not these days — knocked up and preggo, uh uhn. Maybe back when you wore a mullet. These days you got to mind the social habit, the shit going on around you."

"What then, the rabbit died?"

"Not that, no, and no bun in the oven."

"Bun in the oven?"

"More important, it wouldn't hurt you to learn about women," Angel said.

"Guess you're steering me straight, right?"

"Just trying to help."

"And I'm saying the chick goes off, middle of me biting my chalupa — *bam-o*, and slaps me. Hard. You ask me, she needs the help."

"Hormones are some hinky shit, brother, I'll grant you that." Angel looked at him across the table, lowering his voice, the Loop quiet at this early hour. "They get in the family way, and the hormones kick in, and the shit can get real. Why you got to keep to the high ground, my brother. Trust me, I been shacked up enough times . . ."

"Yeah, like how many?"

"Two official, plus one I don't count. But now you're going to tell me you smacked her back, right?"

"In the Taco Bell?"

"Drawing a line in the sand."

"I ever hit this chick, man, they'd be drawing a line around me, doing it in chalk." Cooder sipped again, this fucking awful coffee. Saying, "You don't know Tracy, man. I'm telling you."

"And I'm telling you, brother, it's all about boundaries. Trust me."

"Yeah, hitched two times, and one that doesn't count. Plus, you been switching on Dr. Phil, I bet."

"Fuck that guy, and Oprah too. You ask anybody you want."

"So you recommend an open hand or just give her the full-on knuckles?" Cooder shaking his head, not believing he was in business with this guy thinking he knew women.

"Not saying you do it in the Taco Bell. But I tell you, you don't lay the foundation, next thing you're the whipped dog.

Go on, write it down." Angel went from serious to thoughtful, then saying, "'Less you said something to set her off."

"Like what?"

"I don't know, the something that got you hit."

"Only thing I said, I asked if she's sure it's mine."

"Ah well, there you go." Angel clapped his hands, loud enough he had the bartender looking over.

"What?"

"You think about it. Take a minute."

Cooder grinned back, this guy having his fun. Saying, "So you know women. Been to the plate with your two strikes, plus one you don't talk about. What's that, a bunt?"

"Yeah well, glad I could help." Angel shook his head and glanced around. "Don't know why I'm even talking to you. And what's with the baseball, thought hockey was your game?"

"Six teams and three leagues, being the enforcer. Juvenile and Bantam before that. These days I lace up it's Senior A. Other than that —"

"Yeah, okay. Wasn't asking for your résumé. Look, last thing I'm saying about it, your domestic situation. There's two ways you can go. You stick or you go, understand? One way you wade through shit, the other way you walk through clover. Totally up to you, figure out which way's which. But right now, we got a job. And I need your head in the game. No time for thinking what color to paint the kiddie's room."

Cooder frowned. Not the first job they pulled together, Angel always cocky, playing the man in charge. But he was right on one score, Cooder couldn't let Tracy sidetrack him. Not with this job staring at him.

Looking around the Loop — empty like Valentina told Angel it would be — that transition time between the night before and the morning after. The hour when the gamblers were thinking about hitting the sack instead of cracking the nut. The line of seats along the long bar, a dozen tables and . half dozen booths. Just the red-haired bartender behind the bar. Glass shelves lined with bottles all lit up, every kind of demon drink you could name. Red wiping down glasses with a rag, likely keeping busy to keep from nodding off.

Cooder sipped the shit coffee, bitter and going cold, as bad as the Maxwell House back at Angel's, the place he'd been staying, sleeping on the narrow pull-out in the front room since his release.

After this job, he'd get his own apartment, have some privacy. Robbing this casino guest meant he could afford Vancouver rents. Maybe think about taking things to the next level with Tracy — let her move in and see how it goes. Leaving on the mornings when he stayed over at her trailer, lying he was going to his nine-to-five plumbing job. Tracy with no idea how he made the real money — jacking cars with Angel.

Too much thinking for this hour of the morning. Things had been going his way the last while, the two of them swiping cars and riding dirty, and now, branching into a new kind of felony. Not sure what was coming next, but chances were Cooder was going to die happy and rich — some day far down the line.

His gut was churning with hunger — long time since the chalupa last night, nothing else down there but this shit coffee. He had tried ordering a classic poutine when they came in, the note clipped to the menu calling all dishes six bucks, Red behind the bar telling them the kitchen was closed, Cooder pointing out the menu claimed they served 11 a.m. till late. Red saying that's right, but now wasn't late, it was early. Too early. Just past five o'clock in the morning.

Cooder said there must be some tapas left over, sandwiches, anything on bread; Red shaking his head, giving him the kind of smile that could get a red-haired guy smacked. Cooder saying, "How about a coffee, that be a lot to ask?"

"You want a coffee?"

"Long as you're serving it."

Standing next to him, Angel tapped a foot against the side of his shoe. Cooder making a scene before they even got a table. Angel looking around like he was nervous, likely wondering where this Valentina chick was.

Grinning, Red told Cooder he'd see what he could do, asking if Angel wanted anything. Angel shaking his head.

Cooder slapped five bucks on the bar top, winking to let Red know it was all in fun. What he really wanted was a double Johnny on the rocks, to take the edge off. But he knew tossing drinks on an empty stomach, and doing it ahead of armed robbery, was bad mojo. Knew plenty of guys inside who'd learned that the hard way, guys he met serving his deuce at Kent. A place where you checked your attitude at the gate. A guy like Angel wouldn't last a week in there. Red wouldn't make it a day.

Sipping from the cup, Cooder thinking it's what you get for ordering java in a place serving strong drink, and doing it this time of night. The carafe likely sitting on the warmer since the supper rush, back when he could have ordered tapas.

Valentina was the chick who set this deal up. Angel saying the two of them met in this same bar and hit it off, describing her as a classy knockout. When she asked what Angel did, he was up front, told her he was the jack of cars, luxury division, wore a jacket and tie to work. Told her he was being up front on account she seemed the kind who liked to run with the bad boys.

"That you, a bad boy, with a name like Angel?"

"Maybe you going to find out, girl. I mean, if you're bad enough to handle it."

Took her to dinner at the Flying Beaver, both ordering the butter chicken along with the best bottle in the house, and she laid down her own idea for making easy money, robbing players fresh in town, ones who come to put their money down at the tables, staying at the Rock. Asking him, "That sound like I can handle it to you?"

Angel told her he was in love, hearing her out — the rest of it — how nouveau riche Asians were coming to play. How the tŭ háo were only allowed to take a maximum of fifteen large out of their home country. Chump change to these guys, Valentina telling Angel they found a way around it, money transfers going into a triad account. The players getting on their flights and picking up bags of dirty money as soon as the wheels set down. What RCMP investigators dubbed the "Vancouver model." Players coming to town, using the triad's money, laying the bills down at the tables. The rich having fun, the triad getting their money cleaned, the casinos doing the laundry and raking the profits, getting fat. Nobody complaining.

Valentina spelled out how she'd find a jet-lagged mark flashing hundreds at blackjack, baccarat, roulette, craps, poker, using her body to red-light the man's attention. A cosmo in hand, she'd get him to ask her to dinner at the Hotpot upstairs, sit across from the man and act interested, overlooking the harbor and ordering up some authentic Cantonese, a nice bottle of château something, Valentina leaning forward and showing her world-class cleavage by candlelight, no doubt getting invited up to the man's room. Angel telling Cooder he'd been thinking about it himself, getting her in a room, but so far keeping it professional.

Her plan was simple: let the player get her upstairs. Valentina going along, keeping the man busy till Angel came through the door, make it look like a robbery. Tie them both up, leaving her bonds loose enough so she wriggles free. She'd untie the player and go to the room phone, set to call the cops. Not something the man could let happen. Telling her to hang up.

Later, they'd split the take, half to Angel, half to her. The kind of thing that was too simple to fail. Valentina saying the Rock was lively till two, after that most of the guests would have headed to their rooms, sleeping off the gambling and booze, just leaving a few diehards.

The Loop stayed open round the clock, with its neon over the bar, in case you forgot the name of the place when you called the cab; its banks of lights casting red and blue shadows. Twin widescreens with the sound muted: first screen replaying some grand slam match, one of the Williams sisters going down in straight sets. Cooder watching.

"Wouldn't mind hiking that little white skirt and grand-slamming her into the net, huh?" Angel following his gaze to the widescreen and back.

"Understand what it takes, what she's feeling right now, having played pro myself."

"Comparing hockey minors to world-class tennis, that give you an understanding, huh?"

"Maybe you ought to shut the fuck up."

"Maybe you ought to be thinking what we got ahead," Angel said, his skinny arm going over the seat back, electric-blue linen jacket, yellow silk tie over a black dress shirt, cocking his head to the widescreen. "Need your head in the game, brother."

"You don't know shit."

Angel doing it again, playing the man in charge and getting under his skin. Cooder looked at the other screen, showing a cricket match, looked like primitive baseball, the batsman with pads and that flat bat, and the bowler pitching at the ground, the batsman connecting and the fielder getting the ball and throwing for the stumps.

"You got your mask?" Angel asked.

"Right here, mother." Cooder tapped his jacket pocket. Then he pushed his cup to the middle, thinking what he needed was a smoke. Where did the times go when a man could light up when he felt the need? A capital offense these days, healthy people giving you the stink-eye, signs saying stay fifty feet away. Back in his days in the minors, an after-hours place like this would be blue with tobacco smoke. His cancer-brown pack with the warning on the front, the fucking type bigger than the name: Player's Navy Cut. A shot of a woman in a hospital bed, with tubes coming out of her mouth, the caption reading, "This is what lung cancer looks like." The tobacco companies wheezing and clinging to life. Absent-minded, he reached for his pack, tapped out the last smoke and stuck it in his mouth.

"The fuck you doing?"

Cooder took the smoke out, looked at it and slid it back in the pack. Looking out past the dark wall of windows, the Fraser sludging along, clouds boiling in from the Pacific. Caught himself tapping a shoe under the table, wondering how long before this Valentina showed with the mark.

Taking his arm off the red vinyl seat back, Angel said, "What you make of this carpet?" Pointing to the swirling lines and muddy brown pile. "Thinking Stevie Wonder picked it out."

"We talking about the color scheme now?"

"What I'm doing, I'm making conversation. Saying this place looks like shit."

"If you say so." Cooder looked back to the widescreens.

"By the way, how's the coffee?"

"Ought to try it." Cooder slid the cup across.

Angel grinned. "Sure you're up for this, your mind on it?"

"Kind of thing you ask the weak link. I look like that to you?"

"Got no interest in your link, brother. Believe it. Just making sure you're in the game."

Leaning forward, Cooder was pushing the hat back, catching the motion behind Angel. "That's my thing. I'm always in the game."

Angel half turning to see the woman coming in alone.

"That's her, huh?" Cooder looking at this mid-thirties brunette in a tight red number, cut low and short, all cleavage and thighs. She sat at the bar, between the wide-screens, tennis on the left, cricket on the right. A cool glance Angel's way across a shoulder, then smiling to the bartender and ordering a coffee. Red saying he'd put on a fresh pot. Take him five minutes.

"Yeah, that's my girl, Valentina." Angel said it like he was proud.

"Bet she orders off the menu too."

Valentina giving a look back to the entrance like she was waiting on somebody.

"Girl like that gets what she wants, every time. What we're counting on. Now, drag your tongue off the table, brother. And give it some class, huh?"

Cooder smiled. "Yeah, that's something my link could go for."

"How about you tell your link, crawl back inside. And you act professional."

"Like you don't think about it."

"I don't think, brother, I do. And what makes you think I didn't do already?"

"Meaning you paid her."

"Picked up a dinner tab, is all. The way you do on a date."

Glancing to the bar, Cooder watched her foot play with her pump, the red fuck-me shoes, the red matching her dress.

"You lose your focus, you go from clover straight back to Kent."

No word of a lie in that. Cooder looked back out at the dark, muddy river, dismissing thoughts of Valentina giving him an employee discount, saying, "So where's our boy?"

"Told you, the man flew in first class, from a time zone that's already tomorrow, got all jet-lagged out. And been playing since he touched down, like he can't help himself. Likely cashing in his chips, and be along in a minute."

Cooder made a face.

"Hey, the girl called, told me she had a live one, this Korean guy gambling like it was his last day on earth — up twenty-five grand at blackjack in the first hour. What's that tell you? Carries a Canucks bag stuffed with hundreds. Valentina getting acquainted with the man, finding out he's got lots more cash in his room — tells us to get down here and stand by. That's what we're doing, standing by." Angel giving a casual glance to the bar now, the tennis and cricket still on the screens, Red back to wiping his glasses, making small talk with her. Valentina waiting on her coffee.

"Now it's looking like showtime." Angel saying to Cooder, "That is if you're up for it?"

"Told you I was."

"Cause once we go . . ."

"Keep talking like that, and there's gonna be a new twist." Cooder leaned close, looked at him serious, tired of his attitude.

"Just checking, brother." Angel's smile made it friendly.

"Yeah, mother." Cooder glanced past the bar, saw movement by the doors, a middle-aged Asian guy in a five-grand suit walked across the carpet, a bag with a Canucks logo over a shoulder, walking to the bar. Not alligator, or Fendi, a fucking Canucks bag, looked like it was fat with cash and chips. Cooder taking it as an omen — finally in the big leagues.

Valentina turned and smiled at him, the man sliding onto the stool next to her, kissing her on the mouth. Set the bag down and hooked a Gucci shoe around the strap. Valentina setting her painted nails on his sleeve like hooks, leaning in and giggling at something he said.

. . . *winners and losers*

A ngel came back that first time from seeing Valentina — about a week ago — woke him at two in the a.m., Cooder splayed on the leather pull-out, waking with a start and a stiff neck, closing his mouth and holding his orange fingers before his eyes as Angel switched on the lamp, tossed his keys in the dish, saying, "The fuck's that all over you, brother?" Cooder's fingers Cheetos-orange. "Look like you been doing Tigger."

"Fucking time is it?" Cooder swung his feet off the coffee table, yawning and saying, "So, you bump uglies?"

"Can tell you how I got lucky at the tables. Was down, was up, you know, but hung in and ended on the plus side of flush." He told Cooder about this Valentina he met at the casino, told him she was fine, how he got to know her, finding out she had a recipe for getting rich. "Said she's in need of muscle."

"Telling me you struck out, huh?"

"What I did, I kept it to business, finding out about this recipe. Didn't bring out the muscle. That make you happy?

Not as happy as if I come back here with my pockets turned out, told you I was flat busted and turned down, huh? See you wag that orange finger in my face, saying, 'I told you so.' How I should'a stayed and watched the fucking Idols and ate Cheetos, you and me burping Budweiser. Your kind of night." Pulled a wad of bills from his pocket, Angel dropped it on the coffee table. "Won all the way, brother, and spent time with this fine lady, a knockout, not like what you got, the one you knocked up."

"So you nailed a hooker."

"Man, you don't quit, do you? Her and me are past the meter running. Getting to know each other, talking about business."

"Sounds like you struck out with a hooker."

"You want to hear it, or not?"

Cooder smiled, licked an orange finger, told him to go ahead.

"Knew she was something when I walked in the place, saw her at blackjack, doubling down, not splitting the fives, but doing it on the eights. Not taking the insurance. Winning a hand, then one more. Doing it with style, like she knew what she was doing, you understand. Her legs crossed, the little dress riding high. Smelled good too, like flowers. Looked over at her and said, 'Hey, you on a roll, huh?' Told me she came to win, looking me over, saying, 'How about you?' Like she was taking an interest. I told her I came to score."

Telling Cooder he watched her play a few more hands, the two of them going to the Loop, this Valentina saying over cocktails she had an idea. "Woman wanting me in on it, reaching and fingering my lapel. Says to me, 'Brooks, huh?' Could see I was all about the winning, and asked if I was into making some real money. Told her I was listening."

"Could be setting you up."

"You mean like a cop? Never seen a cop look like that, brother, not in your life. Hiking her little dress, be like entrapment. Good lawyer'd squash a thing like that in about two seconds. And where'd she put the badge?"

"But come on, why you?"

"Why not me?"

"Look, I get you wanting to give her a jump — I mean, sounds like who wouldn't? But some hot chick with a way to make easy money without getting wet . . ."

"Get your head out of the bucket, brother. The woman's got a sweet deal, plain and easy. Needs help pulling it off."

"You tell her you're in show biz or something like that?"

Angel just looked at him, then said, "Me and my lady celebrating ourselves got nothing to do with what I do, or the deal she's talking about, and definitely none of your fucking business, other than I'm telling you 'cause I might let you in. But you rather sit there, lick your Cheetos fingers, falling asleep watching other people living on the TV, that's up to you."

Cooder shrugged. "I got no argument making some extra on the side."

So Angel settled down and laid it out: how Valentina got word from her bartender buddy, pointing out the rollers flying in.

"So what's my bit? Oh, let me guess, I drive?"

"Yeah, but you're right there, backing me up."

"What kind of split?"

"Fifty/fifty, you and me."

"What about her, a finder's fee?"

"No, man, she gets fifty."

"Of the fifty/fifty?"

"You see it's her idea, something she sees as a job for two, her and me. Told her I need you, my wheelman, on account of my eye."

Cooder looking from one eye to the other. "Yeah, can understand that."

"Girl says she hardly noticed, but goes along with you being in the picture, so long as I pay you out of my end."

"So I get the finder's fee."

"We'll hash out the details, brother. Don't you worry."

"And you're gonna do the rough stuff?"

"You making it sound like I can't?"

"I'm saying count me out."

"Don't be like that. This's a good score."

"You want me in, then I do more'n drive. I'm in all the way, right when it goes down, and in for an equal slice after, same as you. This woman's pillow-talking your ass, taking half, with you and me splitting the rest."

"You forgetting it's her play."

"We pull a felony and something goes wrong, and you and me go down hard. She says she had nothing to do with it, wiggles her ass and walks. How about we get a different broad to be bait? Better yet, how about we just stick to what we know?"

"It's called diversifying, brother. Plus, it wouldn't kill us to chill a week or two on the cars. Cops out there're looking for who's been jacking these rich motherfuckers' rides."

Cooder thought about it, then said, "So set it up, but no way it splits in half."

"I'll see what she thinks." Angel looking thoughtful.

"Yeah, when?"

"I'm thinking after," Angel said, guessing Valentina would kick up some fury. Adding, "She doesn't like it, what's she gonna do, call the cops?"

And now Cooder smiled and started nodding.

Angel had to admit it, Cooder wasn't all wrong. Valentina was about the business, but he liked the plan, and he liked her too. They'd hit some guy who couldn't go to the cops, playing with the wrong people's money — not something anybody wanted a light shining on. And maybe Angel and Cooder would slip away with all the cash. The woman believing she'd get half. Angel having his own ideas about it. And had thoughts about Cooder's share too.

Valentina had called the day after they went to dinner, saying, "You know who this is?" Angel saying how could he forget. Valentina said she was tracking a live one. A Korean businessman just flew in from Hong Kong, got himself booked into a suite on the executive floor. Come to play. She'd trolled the tables, catching this guy's eye at blackjack, making his acquaintance, smiled her red mouth at him, her blue eyes saying you're mine. Had a drink with him and gave him an idea of getting her on the king-sized bed, getting on top of her and pumping away his jet lag.

The man's name was Park Won-Soon, Valentina spending the day showing him the best of Lotusland. Got him on a heli-tour over an ice-top, did the Cut Slope, then lunch up on Grouse, cocktails at Hy's — letting the man pay for it all — then went back to his suite and took care of his jet lag.

Angel said to her, "Think it gives me a lift, you saying what you two did?"

"Did it, lift you?"

"We get together later, maybe you gonna find out."

Said maybe she'd save him some, made it sound like a slice of pie. Tonight, she'd be next to Park at the blackjack by nine — the man wanting to play some more, Valentina on his arm like his good-luck trinket. She told Angel the man was walking around with a leather bag, a Canucks logo on it, never let it out of his sight, kept it in a locker when they were up on Grouse. Valentina saying it had to be the laundry. Said she'd call when it looked like he was winding down.

Angel was set to go — thinking how much cash would fill that Canucks bag — told her he'd be waiting on her call.

She told him when they got it done, things could get interesting between the two of them. And let him sit with that.

. . . the hired help

"You win, baby?" Nikki Miller, going by Valentina, smiled and patted his sleeve.

"Number one." Holding up his index finger. The man was Park Won-Soon, told her he was senior operations manager for a company making electronic parts for Hyundai in Seoul. Working out of the Hong Kong office, he was fluent in three languages. Signaling to Red behind the bar, laying down a fifty. Red turning to his bottles, pouring and coming back, sliding a straight scotch in front of him, a vodka martini for her. Took the bill, offering change that Park waved off.

Park offered a toast, saying her name, having a little trouble with the consonants, but not bad.

Valentina said she liked the way he said it, her street name, wanting him to repeat it, smiling when he did. Spearing the stuffed olive from her drink, taking it with her perfect teeth, she chewed it slow, saying, "I got a game for you. You like games, hon? Think you're going to love this one." Sipping her drink, taking her time.

"I'm going to win." Park picked up his glass and sipped too.

"Yeah, can feel a big score coming." Leaning close, she set a hand on his thigh.

Park slapped back the rest of his drink, taking her by the elbow, grabbing the Canucks bag and steering her to the lobby, going to find an elevator.

« « «

The clap on her shoulder from behind had Nikki jumping, the cry caught in her throat. She'd been lost in her thoughts, looking out the floor-to-ceiling glass with a view of the river, not hearing Park step barefoot behind her. The man coming from the shower, a towel around his middle, hair wet and flat, turning her by a shoulder, her hotel robe falling open, a breast showing. He looked at her, and for a heart-beat she thought he'd overheard the call she made to Angel from the balcony, letting him know they were set to go. Gave her a sensation like she was about to be pushed past the sliding doors and pitched over the railing. Learning to fly in seven floors and landing on top of some parked car. Like maybe the man figured her game and knew it was a set-up. Do to her before she could do to him — then go plead diplomatic immunity.

But he was smiling, looking down at her exposed breast, doing that Rick Blaine line, "Here's looking at you, kid."

"Yeah, baby, and look, Ilsa brought a twin." Nikki let the sash go and the robe opened, letting the man look her up and down, Nikki in just the thong and pumps. Smiled when he started touching and kissing.

Getting that heaven-on-earth look, Park slipped the robe off her shoulders, let it fall and turned her around, taking her in with his eyes, then his mouth and hands, his towel falling off — then drawing her tight, kissing her on the mouth and grinding himself at her, dancing her backwards, the two of them dropping onto the bed, the only thing king-size in the room.

"Got over your jet lag, no problem." Patting his boy like it was being good.

Lying back, Park grinned up at her, folding his hands behind his head, watching and wanting her to take him around the world again, saying, "Makes me horny. Makes you horny, too?"

"How could it not." Nikki taking the man to the edge, thinking there ought to be an award, best performance on a king-sized bed — should come with a gold statuette.

Then he pulled her down on him, planted his face between her breasts, started thrusting and grunting till he spasmed. Then it was over and he sunk into the mattress like he'd been deflated. Nikki pretty sure he whispered, "I win, baby."

Took him under two minutes, tops. Getting up, she stepped to the can bare-assed, feeling sorry for Mrs. Won-Soon. Man ought to change his name to Too-Soon.

Not a bad-looking man in an almost-hairless kind of way, not muscular, but at least he wasn't Buddha-round. Not asleep like she hoped when she came out of the can, Park smiling, asking her to call room service, order some oysters and champagne. Wanting to know how long.

Nikki asked into the phone and was told half an hour.

"Time for quickie." His grin was eager. Park with the circus tent going up under the covers.

"Still glad to see me, huh?" Nikki setting the phone down, lifting the covers and getting on the bed, thinking nine o'clock tonight was going to be forever.

« « «

By midnight, Park was up a couple of grand at blackjack, dropped about ten at craps, but having a good time. Then he was hungry again, wanting to take in the buffet. The two of them chowing on excellent all-night West Coast cuisine. Still going strong, the man retried his luck at the craps table, stacking chips on the pass line, playing 3, 7 and 8, avoiding 4, and he racked up a 10G winning streak before finally winding down.

Just past four thirty, Nikki as Valentina went to the little girls' past the casino floor and made another call to Angel, telling him to get set. Said she'd get Park to the Loop for a nightcap, be about five minutes. Brady, the red-haired bartender, fixing her the usual watered drink.

« « «

"Game time." Angel Silva was up, dropping a five spot on the table, nodding thanks to the bartender and walking out, same way Valentina had led the Asian john down the hall just a minute ago.

Snapping up the five, Cooder pocketed it, adjusted the safari hat and followed, not going to pay twice for the same shit coffee, hustling to catch up. Their heels clanking along the tiled floor, the two of them getting there after the elevator door pinged and closed. Angel waited, then pressed the button, knowing they were going to the fifth floor. He got out his mask and got himself set. Just had to get off on five, and find the door propped open by a red shoe.

« « «

Nikki stepped in the bedroom and kicked off her shoes, held them in her hand. Told Park to get himself comfortable while she went to the little girls' again. Couldn't believe he was set to go a third time after a sixteen-hour flight, a day of sightseeing and then playing all night. Must be the Blue Point oysters. Nikki seeing his enthusiasm through the Zegna suit.

Left him standing in front of the king bed, the covers in hotel corners, a half dozen pillows and bolsters at the headboard. Park Won-Soon stripping down to his briefs and socks. Nikki going to the can, out of Park's sight, easing the suite's door open and wedging one of her Michael Kors to keep it from locking, then flushing the toilet, running the water, dropping her other shoe and going barefoot back through the suite.

"You ready, Freddy?" Going to him, letting his hand slip under her dress, moving along her thigh, going for the gates of heaven. Wondering what was taking those guys.

Hadn't liked the idea of Angel needing a second man. She'd laid out her plan and told him no way she wanted anybody else in on it. She saw the split right down the middle. If he didn't like it, she'd get a real man. Angel saying he was more real than she knew, told her how he worked with this guy Cooder every day, a guy he could depend on. Couldn't hurt to have extra muscle and an extra set of eyes. Finally she gave in. There wasn't anybody else she could get, her last man doing seven, second time around for armed robbery, but she hung on to the fifty/fifty, and the extra man was coming out of Angel's end.

She glanced toward the door, the four-inch heel keeping the deal in play. Parting her thighs as much as the tight number allowed, keeping Park busy. The man's fingers clumsy and getting caught in the lacework of her Bordelle, trying to get to the landing strip, the alcohol and jet lag finally catching up. Pulling away from him, she reached behind and tugged down the zipper of her dress, Nikki saying, "Saved some of the real pair-a-dice for you, baby." Stopped herself from taking another glance to the door.

She eased him back on the bed, the guy's briefs hooked between his ankles. Nikki doing a slow strip, pulling the dress off a shoulder.

And they came rushing in, Angel first, his cock-eyes behind a mask, then the big guy behind him, the one Angel called Cooder, his mask not sitting right on his face, a safari hat on his head, tripping on her red shoe, bumping into Angel, the door shutting behind them.

Park shoved her aside, was on his feet, naked, erect, his briefs like convict chains between his ankles. Yelling, "*Haaa!*"

Nikki watching it happen.

Cocking his fist, the big guy pushed past Angel, lobbing a rocket. Angel pulling a piece.

Drunk, jet-lagged and naked, Park ducked to the side, his left hand shooting up, his wrist twisting, deflecting the fist and trapping the big man's arm, jerking him forward, catching him off balance. Park shot a palm strike to the ribs, taking the big man's wind. The hat falling off. Park spearing his fingers for the eyeholes of Cooder's mask. Same time, scraping his foot down the man's shin and stomping his arch. Sending a heel kick at Angel behind him.

Sidestepping it, Angel flipped the pistol in the same motion, came in and swung the barrel as Park missed, catching him on the temple with a melon-thunk, dropping him to the rug.

Nikki was pushing her hips up, trying to get her panties right, then tugging and smoothing the dress.

Taking off the face mask, Angel looked at the man curled on the floor, then at her covering herself up. Thinking he'd never get the picture of her naked from his mind.

"Fuck me." Cooder rose to his feet, shaking his head and blinking, pulling off his own mask, clearing his vision for a better look at her. Then he swung his shoe into the downed man.

Blood dribbled from Park's mouth. His erection a wilting lily. Cooder scooped up his hat, then the bag with the Canucks logo, unzipped it for a quick look inside. Angel going for the wall safe, what they came for.

Nikki grabbing Cooder by the sleeve, wanting to know what took them, giving Angel the override code she got from Red, promising the bartender five hundred bucks for the tip.

Blinking watering eyes, Cooder pulled his arm away, said they hooked left instead of right at the elevator. He kicked his shoe into the downed man's side again, then he smiled at her, saying, "Hey, how you doing? Valentina, right? I'm Cooder."

Said it like a pickup line. Nikki thinking he ought to say something like "Hey, that a bed behind you?" Or "You want me to come stumbling in the room again?"

Angel got the safe open, reached inside and grabbed a leather man-bag, this one Prada, one with a beach scene. Then he was out of there, going down the hall.

"Hey, you forgetting something?" she called.

Cooder kicked at Park a last time, slung the strap of the Canucks bag on his shoulder, pushing past her and going after Angel.

Nikki chased in her bare feet. "Hey, my money!"

Half turning, Angel made the sign of a phone with his thumb and finger, mouthing, "I'll call you." Going for the fire escape.

"For fuck's sakes." Hearing a door slam at the end of the hall, she went back in the room, picking up one pump, sticking it on her foot, the heel with a gouge from being the door stop. Hobbling on the four-inch heel, she got the other one and put it on. Crouching next to Park, careful not to get blood on the Alexander Wang, the red dress setting her back twelve hundred bucks.

The Korean was a mess, blood dripping from his scalp where Angel slugged him. Putting her hand on his chest, checking for a pulse. Unstrapping the Patek Philippe from the slack wrist. A hawk shop on Lonsdale would give her a few hundred for it. Then going to his suit jacket, finding the wallet in the inside pocket. Lifting it, she opened it to gold, black, and platinum cards, a photo of the wife and kids, two hundred and forty in the billfold. Tucking the empty wallet back in his jacket, she patted his chest, saying, "Count yourself lucky, sport. Had a good time, and only cost you two forty and a watch." Looking in the hall mirror, she fixed her hair with her hand, went to the door and looked to the *EXIT* sign down the hall, decided which way to play it, then going back in the room.

. . . maybe I'm doing it wrong

The thought came and went: take his walking stick and swing for the fences, swipe it across the oncologist's desk. Fitch Henry Haut wanted to wipe away that sanctimonious look and watch the doc dive for the floor, then say, "How's that for a man my age?" Never hit a soul who didn't deserve it in seventy-three years, twenty-five of it on the force, but right then, this guy in his white lab coat was begging for it.

Brendan J. Russell, the oncologist, sat with his hands folded, with that practiced manner they taught in med school. The photos angled on the desk, his perfect wife and pair of towhead kids, a jar of jelly beans, diplomas lining the wall, a view of the North Shore mountains out the window. Fitch betting the guy drove a Jaguar.

But all he did was shrug. It wasn't Dr. Russell's fault. Fitch had known about the cancer months before walking into his GP's office, the guy who referred him here. Suspected it when the cough started, and had no doubt by the time he was spitting pink blobs in the sink of his RV. The stabs in his chest and shoulder that woke him every night. Lying in the dark, feeling Annie next to him, Fitch talking to his dead wife, asking her if his colon trouble wasn't bad enough, been hauling around the colostomy bag for the past year. Annie calling him a boob, insisting he pick up the phone and book the appointment. Promising if he didn't, she'd be gone.

When the morning light showed and Annie was gone again, Fitch felt the aloneness come with the dawn. Fearing she wouldn't return the next night, and that was more than he could bear. Annie his constant through all those years of marriage. Never a day without her.

Annie taken away when a cabbie drifted off behind the wheel at the end of a fourteen-hour shift, losing control making the turn at Granville and West Georgia, the Camry crossing the lanes and T-boning her driver's side, plowing her Jetta up onto the sidewalk, right out front of the Bay, the line of commuters at the bus stop scattering. The cabbie walked from the wreckage with scratches, was charged with vehicular manslaughter. In court, the defense lawyer disputed the charges, blaming his client's long hours, the man just trying to make ends meet, competing with the ride-hailers. Blame Uber, blame Lyft, blame the transportation minister. In the end the charges were dropped. And the only consolation, the first responder told Fitch Annie hadn't suffered, his wife gone by the time the ambulance arrived at the scene.

So he hadn't cared much watching the pink blobs slide down his drain, waking to the stabs of pain. Talking to her when it kept him awake, tried to tell her it was nothing, but the Annie of his dreams wasn't buying it. Fitch seeing cancer's bright side, bringing him and Annie back together, sooner than later. She'd be waiting to take his hand, and for right now, he liked that she came back to him most nights.

So he made that appointment with the GP, let the guy put his stethoscope on his chest, listening to his insides, Fitch saying, "*Ahh.*" Getting sent for the lung exam, the GP referring him to Brendan Russell, the oncologist. Russell calling up a chest X-ray, the damned thing showing the shadow at his left shoulder. Russell pointing to it on the light box, saying he didn't like the look of it, not one bit. Fitch saying he didn't care for it much either, telling Russell he never smoked a day in his life, even held his breath walking past busses. Next, Russell sent him for the CT scan. Shaking his head when it came back, showing a mass about three inches wide. Fitch going for a biopsy, the one confirming the lung cancer. Brendan Russell handing him the news from his plump leather, nice view out the window behind him. Told Fitch he could go for a PET, just to be double-sure, but it would be on his own dime. Health Care not covering it these days.

And there he was, in the man's office, looking out at the Lions in snow. Saying, "Never heard a good thing about chemo, doc. Makes people sick, all that radiation, the way I hear it. And to think all this hair's going to fall out?" Running his hand through the silver-gray, thinning a little on top, but not bad for a guy his age.

"Small price to pay, no?" Russell saying there were wig makers.

"Me, wear a rug, you kidding? Go around like Ol' Blue Eyes."

Russell grinned, said Fitch's humor was in good supply. "It means you're a fighter."

"If the chemo misses a few little buggers, these damned cancer cells. Means all your nuking's for nothing, right? And I go from being a fighter to being a landowner, six feet under. Looking good in my toupee."

"Looks like you been reading up?"

"I googled it. Yeah, I can google."

Russell grinned. "Okay, but let's stay positive, Mr. Haut;

let's count on the chemo eradicating all the little buggers, as you put it, okay? Cancer's the enemy here, not the chemo."

"Losing my hair, and yarking up what I eat, what's that, casualties of war?"

"Side effects vary. And appetite returns afterwards, along with the hair."

"Meantime, I'm a guy with no eyebrows . . . even at Walmart, it's going to be weird." Fitch grinned. "Who's gonna love me when the looks are gone?"

"Loved ones tend to stick by you."

"Mine's on the other side, doc. Waiting for me."

"Any kids?"

That felt like a sucker-punch. Fitch saying, "Okay, let's say I go along, and I'm not saying I will, but let's just say . . . when do we start?"

"I'll get you on a waiting list. Mark you down as urgent. Be a month, no more than two, tops. Give you some time to think." Russell gave a sympathetic smile. "Could buy you some good years, Mr. Haut. But without it . . ." He went on and explained about the doses and cycles, laying it out with practiced reassurance.

Fitch wasn't convinced, knowing Annie would nag him to keep his appointments. Threaten not to come back. Even from the far side, the woman possessed the serious mojo she had in life, telling him not to be such a boob.

Fitch looked at the jelly bean jar on the doc's desk, the photo of the guy's wife and kids. Russell glancing at his desk clock, saying, "So how about it, Mr. Haut, let's get you booked in?"

Fitch rose from the chair, put his weight on the walking stick. "How long if I skip it?"

"Without the chemo . . ." Russell sighed. "Maybe four, six months tops."

"How about remission?"

Russell leaned back in his chair. "You heard the one about two chances, slim and none?"

"The one where slim leaves town?" Fitch nodded and started to turn for the door.

Russell said, "Either way, if you haven't done it, be a good time to consider a living will."

Fitch thanked him, this man with his nice wife and kids, likely had a house in Altamont, driving a damned Jag, teeing off at Quilchena, sucking oysters at the Blue Water. All that and the man couldn't work miracles. Fitch turned for the door, saying, "Could get a second opinion."

"Be happy to refer you," Russell said, sounding like he didn't take it personal. "Of course, it could mean more tests, money and time . . ."

"Yeah, yeah, time." Taking his crutch, Fitch left the office, shuffled past the blonde with the Dagmar bullets at the reception desk, smiling to her and getting out of there, wondering if Russell was getting a taste of that, a little tarnish on the perfect life. That cynical attitude that followed him from the force into old age, something that would get Annie scolding him. Stepping on the elevator, he couldn't get out of the med building fast enough. Breathing the street air, thick as soup with the fumes of the Lower Mainland. No big wonder city people got cancer.

But he'd had a good run, seventy-three years' worth. Stepping aside on the sidewalk for a lady pushing a stroller past him. The woman thanking him and turning up the walk to the medical building, telling him to have a nice day.

"I got no complaints," he said.

"Must be nice," she said and pushed on.

Fitch watched the woman, about his own age, pushing the stroller, and he was thinking he ran out of nice days when that idiot cabbie fell asleep at the wheel, taking Annie. Going to his parked RV. "Happy Camper" on the spare tire cover on the back. Back to thoughts of crossing over, taking comfort in it. No pain and no getting older over on that side. The side where he'd be holding Annie's hand again, soft and gentle in his. Pictured her the way she was the day they got hitched, the confetti in their hair, him guiding her by the hand down the steps and into the back of the rented Rolls.

Later he might pop some Orville, haul the old Bell & Howell from the back of the cupboard, pin the bedsheet across the kitchen cubby and project Super-8 memories, relive days with Annie and Carolyn growing up in Kodak color.

Stepping along the street into the RV's shade on the passenger side. The thirty-foot Winnebago Brave taking up two spaces. Fishing keys from his pocket, he shifted his weight on the walking stick and opened the handle lock, switching back the dead bolt. Using the stick, he stepped into the only home he had to get in order.

His mind on their wedding night, that first time, every detail of it. Feeling her against him, catching her breath under him. The only woman he'd ever been with. Wondering if his old fella could still attempt a salute. Could hear Annie saying something like, "My my, what have we here?" That smile of hers, then, "Be a shame to waste it."

Getting in, he snapped off the disabled parking tag hanging from the mirror. Saying to it, "That sound handicapped to you?" Tossing it on the dash.

« « «

Driving back to what the boondockers dubbed Tin Pan Alley, the vacant land surrounded by Harbourside, he was whistling "Heartaches," an oldie by the Ted Weems

Orchestra, Fitch's poor attempt to chirp like Elmo Tanner did on the old 45. Always made Annie laugh, him puffing air past his lips, more wind than whistle, and no way he could hold a tune to save his life.

Changing lanes, going eastbound on Marine Drive, he looked at the guy in the mirror, still whistling, deciding there would be no chemo. He was thinking of driving to the Okanagan and spend what time he had with Carolyn, try not to let the old get in the way. Always a chance of remission — something to baffle Russell and the rest of the white coats — Fitch living long enough to hold Carolyn's baby, knowing his grandchild's name, its little fingers wrapped around one of his.

The news gave him time to come up with a bucket list, something his buddy Milton Byrd and the fellas had talked about over pinochle, the boondocking boys getting together on weekend evenings, sitting and doing some trick-taking, a couple still drinking the hard stuff, the rest going with herbal tea or Boost. The old boys talking about what they'd still like to do, most of them fooling themselves.

And no need to return that dry bureaucrat's call, the Fleming woman at BC Housing with her civil-servant voice, leaving a message for him about the rent subsidization he was eligible for, a one-bedroom in a seniors' residence becoming available over by False Creek. Been waiting his way to the top of the list for the past two years. Always knowing he'd have to give up the boondocking life sooner or later.

Turning right on Fell, he promised himself he wouldn't become a burden on his daughter, glad he wasn't going to end up in that home where old folks went to wait to cross the Styx, eating food with no salt, drinking thickened liquids designed to keep the inmates from drooling on themselves.

A place where Jell-O was the high point of any meal — hell, the high point of the whole day.

Driving past where First met Second, Fitch was whistling "This Guy's in Love with You."

Born the year after the jackboots stomped hell across Europe. He'd been around since before the polio vaccine. Had seen the first primetime broadcast, that CBC butterfly in color. Growing up in Toronto's Junction, big into street hockey when the first subway rumbled under Yonge Street in '54, only a dozen stops on that first leg. The same year Hurricane Hazel knocked the roof off his parents' two-bedroom place. Holding the wood ladder for his old man as he trudged up with the bundles of shingles and flopped them up onto the roof. Handing him roofing nails from the Aikenhead's bag. Remembered being allowed to stay up late enough to catch Steve Allen. Remembered Sputnik and its deep *beep-beep*, orbiting till its batteries ran out, and firing up the Cold War. And he remembered Elvis from the waist up, something that got most women jumping and screaming. Fitch had combed his hair like that, hoping for sideburns someday, anything to get some female notice. Sitting in class when the announcement came that Kennedy rolled topless through Dallas, causing nations to weep. All of that long-ago still clear in his mind, sometimes feeling like it all just happened.

Parallel parking behind an Evo rental car, he took another glance in the rearview. Long time since he'd rocked the pomp. Had the sideburns by the time Annie said yes, the two of them getting hitched at the Gladstone, a swank place on Queen, a year before Carolyn was born.

Holding her in his arms, tiny and red-faced, the three of them living in that flat on Roncesvalles. Carolyn blowing out four candles the year he went to serve his country, Canadian forces helping to stabilize the Congo. A six-month tour as a signaler, sporting a crewcut by then, minus the sideburns. Joined the RCMP when he got back, did his cadet training at Depot.

Sat with Annie and Carolyn five rows back of the net when Mahovlich scored a couple in Game 2 of the Summit Series, everybody jumping at the Gardens. The three of them on their sofa when Henderson tucked in the goal of the century, with thirty-four seconds left in Game 8. Felt the pride when Terry Fox laced up for the Marathon of Hope. Won dugout seats when the Jays won the World that first time. Taking the promotion and being transferred to Cloverdale, the three of them living on Canada's West Coast.

A lot of living in the rearview, and Fitch had no regrets. The only thing he had for his bucket list was getting back to Peachland, spend time with Carolyn and her baby. Reaching for the phone to call her when it dawned on him, it was meatloaf day, the Tuesday special at the Potlatch, his weekly indulgence. Nearly slipped his mind after getting the verdict from Russell. And today, he was going to double up on the buttered garlic bread.

. . . *lying low*

C areful when she poked her head above the roofline, looking all around. She moved to the next row of cars, walking easy and trying to pass for a dumb kid who forgot where her dad parked. Checking door handles, Wren McKenna was hoping to find one unlocked before the clouds ripped, the rolling dark and gray overhead, the wind picking up as temperatures dropped. The early morning had her shivering inside the hoodie.

And there it was, the open door. Lifting the handle and giving another look around, she opened it enough to get in, closing it behind her, getting the dome light to shut off. Rubbing her hands together, she checked around the interior. Some kind of SUV, what her mom would have called a stupid ugly vehicle, the linger of stale smoke inside. Likely belonged to guests of the casino hotel, sleeping in their room. Hoping to wait out the worst of the rain, long enough to stop her teeth from rattling.

Without the ignition key, she couldn't switch on the heater, longing to hold her hands in front of the warm blowing air. A fine rain speckled the windshield, the glass fogging up, something that would give her away. Wiping at it with her sleeve, she felt under the seat, then checked the glovebox, hoping for something to eat or anything she could use. Touched something under the seat that felt like gum, and she stopped checking, wiping her hand on the carpet next to the floor mat.

The rain pecked harder, a steady beat on the roof. Climbing between the seats, she pressed buttons but couldn't get the side window open to keep the glass from fogging. She pulled up her knees on the rear bench, crossing her arms and tucking her hands underneath. Getting drowsy, she tipped to the side, not wanting to drift into a heavy sleep, keeping her head against the side glass, telling herself, "Just for a few minutes."

Not sure how long it had been, snapping awake when she heard the voices, the gray sky lighter now, morning starting to break. First thought, the rain was playing tricks, tapping the roof, but the rain had stopped, and the voices were coming closer. Could get out the rear door and run, but she decided to wait, getting behind the rear seat and down on the floor. Her heart pounding out of her chest.

The sound of a remote fob, the locks clicking, the SUV rocked as a man got in the driver's side, another man getting in the passenger side. Wren hoping they didn't hear her heart beating.

"You see that dude go down?" the one on the passenger side said, laughing. Reaching a pack of smokes, he handed the driver one and pushed in the dash lighter. "Come on, man, let's get the fuck gone. Go and count this shit."

"It look like I'm doing something else?" The driver started the engine. Tires chirped, and they were rolling out of there, hopping the driveway lip and getting onto River Road.

The passenger said, "How about lighten up, Cooder? And think about what I got here." Clapping a couple of bags on his lap. "Fucking score of a lifetime."

"What d'you mean, what you got?"

"What I got from the guy you tried to drop, except you didn't. Me jumping in and getting what we came for. But hey, don't worry about it."

"Hey, Angel . . ." Giving him the finger, the one called Cooder saying, "Thanks for the pep talk." Then blaming the stupid masks Angel insisted on, the thing getting twisted on his face, blocking his vision.

"Yeah, well, turned out in the end." Tapping the bags again, Angel took the cigarette lighter, lighting Cooder's, then his own. Both of them puffing.

"Didn't need you doing shit. Was getting it done," Cooder said.

"Except when the guy was kung-fu'ing your ass. Doing it in front of my girl too."

"Your girl?"

"The one didn't want you in in the first place. Guess I got some explaining to do, but like I said, it's no big deal."

"The big deal's you going on about it, talking like you saved my ass."

"How'd you put it?"

"The fucking masks."

Turning her head, Wren looked at the lever handle on the rear gate, figuring how to open it. Telling herself to wait for the first red light. Jump out when they stopped and run the opposite way as fast as she could. If they came after her, it would take them a minute to turn this big thing around. Hoping these guys weren't fast, knowing smokers weren't good at running.

Cooder drove along River Road, slowing for an amber light.

Angel saying, "What the fuck you doing now?"

"What, driving too slow?"

"Well, was me, I would've jumped the light."

"Yeah? You mean like . . ." Cooder stomped the pedal, the Expedition blasting through the red, accelerating as they crossed the bridge.

Wren felt herself knocked into the tailgate, her heart in her throat, hoping they hadn't heard.

Pointing out the one-way, Angel was wondering why he was taking the Grant McConachie, heading west and having to loop back, just to go north in the end.

"Was a no-turn back there, in case you missed it."

"Yeah, but nobody's around."

"So you want me drawing attention." Swinging them onto the Arthur Laing, Cooder making a wild lane change.

"The fuck you doing?" Angel holding tight, glaring at him.

"These fucking signs." Cooder slowed to the speed limit, trying to make sense of the signs and arrows.

"Yeah, can't be the driver, that's for sure."

"How about you enjoy the scenery and shut the fuck up?" Cooder sounding angry.

"Hey, it my fault the little guy did you like that? And all I'm doing here is being the extra eyes."

"You mean mouth. Your extra eye, the cock-eyed one's worth shit. Why I'm driving in the first place."

The two of them puffed, smoke collecting at the head-liner, neither opening a window. Wren feeling her stomach turn.

Angel saying, "What was that, kung-fu you think? Fast, I'll give him that."

"Just be the extra eye, okay? I wanted to hear lip, I could've brought the old lady. Which reminds me . . ." Cooder taking out his cell, punching in a number.

"The one you knocked up, calling her the old lady now?"

Giving him a look, Cooder getting no answer, putting the phone back in his pocket, then he wheeled onto Granville, clicked on the oldies FM, Bachman–Turner taking care of business, booted it over the bridge over Southwest Marine, got caught at the light at Sixty-Seventh.

Wren hesitating now, not daring to look up, missing the chance to jump.

Glancing at the signage on a building, thumping his thumbs against the wheel, Cooder sounding impatient for the light to change. "That a restaurant or bank?" Said he couldn't tell from the Asian lettering out front.

"Fuck's it matter?"

"Can't tell if I make a deposit or order out." The light changed, and Cooder gave it some gas.

"That racial shit make you feel better?" Angel said, shaking his head, dragging on his smoke.

"Just saying I could eat."

"Was an Asian guy made you tap out, then made you rich."

"Could go for some wontons."

"You know it's breakfast, right?"

"That's when they eat it, wontons."

"That so?"

"Had an uncle got his ticket punched in Hong Kong, a sergeant major in the Winnipeg Grenadiers."

"Taught you about eating Chinese?"

"Man married a gal from over there. When he died, she moved here and stayed with my folks. Man, the grub she cooked up. Makes me water, thinking about it."

49

"Wontons for breakfast, huh?"

"And these pancakes she made, forget what she called them. Mustard pickles, spicy sauce on the side, *mmm* man, the best chow I ever had."

"So your uncle the grenadier, that like the guys guarding the palace, the red jackets and big hats?"

"Not a bit like that. I'm talking about the time of WW2, the big one." Cooder tapped his cigarette at the ashtray, saying, "One of the Canadian boys sent to beef up this garrison, middle of the Pacific. Most of the time playing cards, peeling potatoes and cleaning carbines, till the night they got bushwhacked. Overrun by superior forces is what the official report called it. A clusterfuck of bullets going this way and that. My uncle holding his ground, but doing it too close to the guy who threw himself on the grenade."

"His wontons going everyplace, huh?" One side of Angel's mouth going into a smile. Good eye looking out the window.

"Whole squad got taken out that day, that funny to you?"

"Naw, not a bit. Sorry, man. Go on." Angel still looking out the window.

"Got a citation, the man giving it up for his country and getting decorated for it. Felt the pride growing up as a kid, you know, seeing that cross of valor in the glass case on the mantel. My old man proud too, talking about his brother, showing the spot on the globe, the one that came with the encyclopedias."

"Still got it, the medal?"

"Folks sold the place back in the boom, downsized before the old man got put in the home. Not sure who got the medal, the encyclopedias too. Relatives plundered through the place. Just know he was a true patriot, buried over there, some place called Sai Wan Bay. Did it so guys like you and me can go walking around free."

"Free to rob the offspring of the guys who tossed the grenade?" Angel shook his head, mashing the butt in the ashtray.

"You're an asshole, you know it?"

"No offense, brother. I feel your loss." Angel giving a salute. "And thank you for his service." He rolled his eyes and reached his pack, offered it to Cooder. Pressing in the lighter.

"You got somebody like that, stood up and served?"

"Yeah, my cousin Freddy."

"Yeah, when was this?"

"Right now." Angel pulled the lighter, put it to his smoke, saying, "Serves at the Moonglow, take-out joint in East Van. Trouble is they don't open for breakfast, or we could swing by. But if you're ever around, go for the móh-gū gāi-pin. You know what that is? Eat it with the little sticks. Yeah, love how they do it with the snow peas." Angel puffed, and they were quiet a minute, the Expedition rolling north.

"That true, about your uncle?" Angel said, pressing a button, getting his window to roll down.

"Every word. And true, I'm hungry, so you see some place with a drive-thru, let me know, these signs nobody can read."

"Ought to pick up a history book sometime. Learn about cultures that make up this place." Angel puffed smoke, blew it out the window. "Assuming you can read."

"How about you, you read with that eye? Like two pages at once."

On the floor in back, Wren weighed her chances of grabbing the handle again, pushing it up and jumping out the back. Not sure where they were now, but guessing from the tall buildings they were driving through downtown.

Could be the best place to bail. Harder to chase her in a gridlock, and lots of people with cell phones, happy to snap pics of two guys chasing a kid.

Not sure what these two were into, but she knew it was bad. And getting caught would be worse. The smoke filling the vehicle was getting to her, Wren squelching a cough. Something telling her again to wait, not to jump out yet.

"How much you think?" Angel hefted one of the bags on his lap. "Could do a quick count."

"Gonna wait till we get there." Cooder put his arm out, stopping him. "Two of us'll do it, like we agreed."

"Could be we're fleeing with the man's laundry."

"So we'll find out at the same time."

"Guess you figure I'll go all Penn & Teller on you, huh? Make the cash disappear."

"I get distracted behind the wheel, two of us gonna go Villeneuve. At least get the attention that gets us jammed up." Cooder kept driving, keeping it to the speed limit. "Why we're gonna wait."

Pressing the window back up, Angel shrugged like it made sense, still dragging on his smoke.

Cooder finally saying, "How about the chick?"

"Valentina, yeah, a nice piece of ass, right?"

"You gonna take care of her? Her share, I mean?"

"You just worry about the one you knocked up."

They were quiet a time, Angel puffing and looking out at the city coming awake with the morning. The Expedition rolling onto the Lions Gate, the North Shore slopes up ahead, the lights showing at the top of Grouse.

Offering the pack, Angel pushed in the lighter again, saying, "You see the dude's face when I popped him, saving your ass. Man's eyes rolled back like a pinball, sounded like cracking a coconut."

Cooder pinched another smoke from the pack, saying, "Only thing got saved was him from a worse beating."

"Come on, how many stitches you figure I put on him?"

Cooder shrugged like it didn't matter.

Angel took the lighter when it popped and lit them both up, puffing his smoke to life. Saying, "One thing's sure, that dude's going back to wherever-land and telling his old lady this postcard town's got some bite. No way he's coming back here."

Cooder nodded, knowing what Angel hadn't told him about the Vancouver model. Rich Asians coming to play, but only allowed to take so much cash from their own country, getting around it by transferring money to a triad account while still at home, and picking up some playing money once they landed at YVR. How dirty cash got cleaned. Any windfall the players made at the tables stayed here. Players buying up property on the coast. Driving up the values with their laundered cash, something they couldn't explain back home. Cooder thinking the guy they robbed got what was coming. Then asking, "So, how about the chick? She's back there thinking she's getting half?"

"Told you I'll take care of it."

"Gonna screw her over, aren't you? Not even a finder's fee."

"I'm not there yet."

"And if she goes to the cops?"

"A woman like that going to the cops. You hear yourself?"

"So you're screwing her over?"

"Said I'll take care of it."

"Or she goes to the guys doing the laundry, an outfit likes to cut throats."

Angel waved his smoke around, looking surprised Cooder figured it out. Saying, "Except she's in on it. Be the first to get her little throat cut."

"Think we just go back to jacking cars, what we know."

"Man, listen to you worrying your mind — and with a kid on the way."

"Hear they're into that slow slicing, call it a lingering death."

"You google that, letting your mind run wild."

"Google it yourself, how the triad takes a blade and slices under your skin, keeps doing it in layers. Treating you like pastrami till they get tired of you screaming."

"Yeah, okay, screaming pastrami, I'll check it out." Angel looking at him, saying, "Okay, I'll get us squared with my girl, then we'll go back to jacking rides." Clapping his hand on the bags, saying, "But how about first we see what we got?"

"Soon as we get back." Cooder drove through town, people getting ready for another day of nine-to-five. Turning the Expedition onto West Georgia, driving through the park and across the Lions Gate, a freighter passing under the bridge, the city-bound lanes packed with commuters.

Not sure where they were now, Wren lay still, felt the bridge tremble under the wheels, felt the sway as they turned into North Van, driving east along Marine.

"What say to Tim's, get something to go?" Cooder saw the sign ahead, beating an amber light.

Angel said he wasn't big on breakfast, stamped out another butt, sticking a fresh one in his mouth. Cooder saying he could do with a couple of those biscuit breakfasts, along with a decent cup of joe. "Still got the taste of shit coffee, that red-headed fuck serving it — who knows what he put in there — fucking attitude."

Angel pressed the lighter, the ashtray packed with butts. "Rule one: never piss off a server."

"Getting crowded in there, huh?" Cooder glanced at it, too full to close the lid.

"Yeah, get my housekeeper right on it."

Cooder gave him a look.

Pulling out the ashtray, Angel pressed his window down and shook out the ashtray, some of the ash blowing past his seat into the back. Clipping the ashtray back in, saying, "There you go."

The two of them looking at each other.

That's when she coughed, both men jumping, then turning in their seats, Cooder stomping the brakes hard, grappling with the steering to keep it in the lane.

Grabbing the strap handle as the vehicle screeched to a halt, Wren jerked it up, and the lift-gate sprang open, and she jumped out, her feet pounding the pavement, across the intersection, dodging cars in the lane. A van coming up on the inside screeched and honked, and she jumped past it as it jerked to a stop, the woman driver's eyes wide. From there she was running blind. Not looking back. Pounding her feet, rounding the first side street, past some place selling rocks and minerals, then ran into an alley, past a dumpster, some homeless man huddled behind it, looked like he was going to the toilet. Darting along the next side street, a park at the end of it, racing along a footpath and crossing a footbridge over a creek. And she kept going past the back end of another mall, going till she felt the stitch in her side.

. . . a little help from above

P arking in the shade of a boulevard hornbeam — good for another three hours of parking before he had to move it again — Fitch hauled out the folding rocking lounger, dragged it across the road on the garage creeper, his thermos balanced on top. The North Shore mountains and the Winnebago at his back. The flying *W* with the faded red and orange stripes from front to back. A touch of rust starting to show along the passenger window frame, Fitch thinking of it as RV cancer, and from the look of it, it was in stage two. Meaning his rig would outlast him.

Vintage when he bought the old girl on the wrong side of the millennium, he loved the purr of the big-block 440 Dodge, toned like it was echoing all those miles of memories. Had the roof air, a three-burner cooktop, the sofa bed at the tail end, fold-down dinette/bed in mid-cabin, and all the storage a man could want.

Carolyn just a kid back when he bought it. Annie packing them up, and Fitch piloting to Nelson, the three of them visiting relations on Annie's side, then pushing through to the Rockies, Banff and Jasper, up to Swan Lake and Seven

Sisters. Good times on those summer trips, back when summer camping with Mom and Dad was a cool thing for Carolyn, when the Brave was up for those long hauls, not blowing smoke or overheating or giving mechanical grief. Fitch forgiving her for it now, age just something that caught up with everything, even Winnebagos.

Sipping his coffee, he felt the early sun on his skin. Breathing the sea air and rocking on his strip of heaven, the patch of boulevard lawn with the million-dollar view along the Spirit Trail walkway, and no grass to mow. Early snow showing at the Lions and up on Grouse, the Eye of the Wind turning at the top. Fitch never taking the sights for granted, taking in as much of it as he could until quarter past eleven, then he'd drive over to the Potlatch — be there for the start of the lunch special. He could already taste the meatloaf. Along with that garlic bread covered with butter.

Sitting in this spot, where he passed many an afternoon with his boon buddy Milton, retelling tales and arguing which rig ruled: Winnebago or Triple E. Milton's pride and joy sat parked across the open field. Milton and Minkie calling it home, along with their wiener dog, Bullitt. Minkie's idea, ordering Milton to get himself a dog, get him out walking every day, good for his ticker. Milton's idea was why walk when you can drive, so he got a dog with stubs for legs, one that loved the lounge over the leash. This spot being the farthest Milton and Bullitt liked to walk, bringing a thermos of his high-octane tea, what Minkie, up to now, thought was plain Tetley's. Captain Morgan helping to take the chill off this time of year. A pocket of Milk-Bones for Bullitt.

Pouring the last of the coffee from his own thermos, Fitch replayed the visit to Russell's office. The worst news a guy could get, but aside from the idea of the increasing pain, he was okay with the end coming. Annie would be at those gates, waiting for him, telling him something like, "Wipe your feet before you come in."

Rubbing a thumb at something in his eye, he blinked it away, looking across at the Living Shangri-la and the twist of the Trump rising over downtown, the sun glinting on the round top of Harbour Centre to the east. The sails of Canada Place at Coal Harbour, the *Pacific Princess* docked alongside, the last of the cruise ships set for its repositioning cruise.

Milton had scribbled it at the top of his bucket list: take Minkie on what he called one of those Disney ships and cruise up to Alaska. See some glaciers and orcas, step off at Anchorage, humoring the woman and doing the box-step under the stars, all the all-you-can-eat and drink any man could want.

The gray over the city was rain, the mass making a slow roll to the east, looking like it would miss the North Shore. A float plane was coming in low over the water, slicing into the waves and taxiing to the seaplane terminal. A couple of the pinochle crowd had gassed about chartering a prop plane to fly them over the Gulf Islands, looking down at this land of God. Scribbling it on their bucket lists.

Hadn't been this gray since the smoke blew in from the fires in the Fraser Valley, blazes that claimed thousands of acres, smoke hanging like a cloud bank over the city, the whole place smelling like a campground. During the months when the harbor seals sunned on the pilings of what had been the King's Mill logging operation. The eagle's nest empty in the top of the tallest of the trees across the field, more of it showing as the autumn leaves fell. Fitch missed the high-pitched cries of the eaglets, the brood always hungry. The adults winging in search of food, tormented by crows and gulls. The eagles about as welcome by the local wildlife as the boondockers were by the decent taxpayers.

Locals dubbed this spot south of Marine as Tin Pan Alley. And folks like Fitch in their rusting motor homes were boondockers, regarded as the homeless on wheels, only moving on when they were forced out, going to find someplace else to pull up. And the posted development signs on the vacant land promised another glut of condos were on the way, city council hungry for those tax dollars. Meaning the boondockers would get pushed out soon enough.

Fitch had handed the keys to the house in Peachland to his widowed daughter, Carolyn, after Annie passed, the house where she grew up, the place too quiet for him. Packing up the Brave, he got on the Crowsnest and drove west to visit Milton and Minkie, blowing out the tailpipes. Catching a tailwind, he got seven or eight to the gallon on the rebuilt Dodge, making the drive in a day.

He made one more run back last June. Fitch standing in the rented suit in the hundred-degree heat, witness to his kid brother, Eugene, receiving last rights. Just hit seventy and a pulmonary artery put him a few plots over from Annie's. Standing among family members half his age, he laid flowers by Eugene. Another bouquet for Annie, cleaning her plot of weeds and stones, Fitch feeling like the last of his generation, the last man standing, his own shadow growing longer. The empty plot between Eugene and Annie waiting for him. Then he got in the Brave and drove off, back to being nobody from somewhere.

Rocking the lawn chair now, he watched a power couple walking their two greyhounds, going past the beach volleyball court to the fenced area where the dog crowd slung tennis balls with those plastic launchers, standing around and talking about pedigrees and vet bills. Knowing each other by their pets' names. Sometimes Fitch would walk over and somebody would cast him a wary look or a quick hello.

Could be that looking at this old-timer reminded them of what lay ahead. The dogs were always happy to stop and pass the time — they never judged, always eager to get a pat, hoping for a biscuit.

Old and in the way, he was getting his ticket punched: once a husband, a father, officer of the law who'd served in the military, and the guy who held down the fort. Fitch telling himself it had been a life well-lived, and he had no complaints.

It was the two guys driving past in the Expedition that got him turning his head and held his attention. Pulling into the empty spot up from the Brave. The blond one getting out from behind the wheel was a big man, the one getting out of the passenger side was a smug-looking guy, about a hundred and forty pounds, the kind with shoes with lifts.

Watching them cross the road, talking in hushed tones, looking around and heading toward the dog park, but with no dog. Both glanced around like they were guilty of something. Fitch thinking they ought to work on their Doris Day looks, keep from drawing attention.

If he wasn't on his own way out, Fitch might start flipping the latch on the RV's door at night. Didn't matter — nobody in their right mind would break into something like the Brave — the most valuable thing in the place being Stouffer's, two entrees stacked in the ice box, but who said these guys were in their right minds? Maybe he'd just been a cop too long, looking at people with a jaundiced eye.

Advising his neighbors not to leave cash or anything of value in plain view, and not to hide their goodies in obvious spots like cookie jars and sock drawers. And to avoid the ATMs — this part of the city getting too sketchy for the gray-hairs to be cashing pension and old age security checks at a machine, with their backs to the street.

Fitch kept his lettuce in a savings account at the Royal. What he needed day to day stayed in his hip-leather. Opposite the colostomy bag, bulges that made him look wider than he was. He didn't live in fear, more by the basics, putting on his specs and scanning the Walmart flyer, in the habit of stretching a dollar. Checking for deals on Dinty Moore and Chef Boyardee. The Intenso pods for the Nespresso were an indulgence, and once a week he'd treat himself to a drip at Bean Around the World. And he was getting better at making a bag of Werther's last more than a week.

Quarter after eleven when Fitch set the folding chair and thermos back on the creeper and stowed them inside, set to haul the twenty-one-footer to the Potlatch. You get diagnosed with terminal cancer, it means you get to eat all the garlic bread you want. Fitch forgetting about the lean diet, not fretting today about the pain and diarrhea that may come on account of his faulty colon. Today, he'd have butter dripping from his fingers.

Getting behind the wheel, he realized he wouldn't need to worry about moving the Winnebago every four hours anymore. The boondockers making an RV ballet of it, jockeying around the empty field, switching parking spots by more than a hundred feet, avoiding the fines. Bylaw enforcement cutting them some slack, slow to tug out the ticket books on these aging campers, usually letting them off with a warning. As long as the boondockers didn't leave trash or draw noise complaints, the City of North Van turned a blind eye, even put a porta-potty at the bottom end of Harbourside, and stocked it with double-ply. Compliments of the bureaucrats.

But the hoarding had gone up this past summer, the city granting approval for land development, meaning luxury condos were set to blight the landscape and suck up the views and public spaces, meaning the boondockers would be shoved off once ground was broken. A few months and they'd all have to find new squatting grounds. The dozers and earth movers were coming, digging their ugly holes. Concrete and beams would go in and units would go up with multimillion-dollar views to downtown, laminate floors, granite countertops and soaring ceilings. A concierge in the lobby. Parking underground for the Beemers and Benzes of the tax-paying residents who wouldn't abide with rusting eyesores lining their block. The same city officials who'd turned blind eyes would send bylaw enforcement, taking a new viewpoint, letting the boondockers know it was time to push on. And they'd find someplace else. But for Fitch, none of it mattered. He was shuffling off to Peachland, likely right off this mortal coil before they broke earth.

Then he was watching the two men coming back, both still looking around, arguing as they got to the black SUV, the smaller one raising his voice, complaining that the kid heard them talking about the money.

... *poking at shadows*

Soon as the kid jumped out, Cooder squeezed to the curb, motorists giving him a look, a kid jumping out and running from the back of a tinted Expedition. Cooder not looking over, just sat with his hands gripping the wheel, acting natural.

"I got this." Angel stepped out, smiling and shaking his head, putting on a kids-these-days look for the other motorists, walked to the back and shut the lift-gate, threw up his hands like *What's a parent got to do?* Stood with his hands on his hips for a second, watching the kid with the backpack running away. A woman in a Nissan frowned a look of sympathy, buying his act. Looking at his watch like the kid would be late for school, he walked in the direction the kid had run off, out of sight now around the next corner. He kept up the show. Thinking at least the kid wasn't screaming.

"Fuck me," Cooder muttered, watching Angel in the side mirror, guessing what it must look like. If anybody snapped a pic with their cell and called the cops, he'd be fucked, sitting in a stolen ride with bags of cash on the passenger floor.

Putting it in gear, he rolled, Angel walking the opposite way, in the direction the kid had gone.

Pulling onto Pemberton, he turned into the Mickey D's lot, found himself in the drive-thru lane, rolling down his window, putting it in neutral — thinking what to do — till the car behind him honked for him to pull up, a young guy, the kind of hair that said *Punch me in the face*, leaning out his window, calling to him, "Keep the line moving, huh, buddy."

If it wasn't for the mounting shit, Cooder would have got out and walked back, leaned in the guy's window. Pulling to the squawk box, Cooder rolled down his window. A girl's tinny voice asking for his order.

"How about a McDouble."

"We're serving breakfast, sir."

The guy behind revved his engine, letting him know he was in a hurry.

"Look kid, you take a frozen patty, slap it on the grill. How hard is that?"

"Breakfast's till ten-thirty, sir."

Looking at her a long moment, Cooder considered before saying, "How about you do me one of them bagels?"

"Just what's on the menu, sir."

The guy behind him tapped his horn, some kind of rap music pumping from his car stereo.

"Have to back up to see it, and I got this dude on my butt . . . Look, kid, just a bagel, egg, sausage, cheese. Surprise me, okay?"

"That be a sausage 'n egg bagel, sir?"

"Yeah, that'd be nice. How about make it two."

"You want the bagel plain?"

"Whatever you think."

"And a coffee with that, sir?"

"Hell, no." Cooder still dealing with the swill at the casino, his stomach complaining.

The guy behind revved again.

The tinny voice gave him a total, asked him to drive to the next window.

"In a sec." Cooder got out, walked back and thumped a fist on the hood of the kid's car, went to the open window and said, "Do it again."

"What?" The guy reeling away.

"Honk or rev your engine, either one."

"Come on, man, I got places to be."

"That right?"

Cooder looked at the car behind this guy's, some woman busy with her cell phone.

"That music you got on?"

"Yeah?"

"You got any Motörhead?"

"A what?"

"Play shit like that, and you gonna taste a McSlappie."

"A what?"

And Cooder backhanded him through the open window, told him if he heard that shit again, he'd super-size it, then walked back to the SUV, left the guy sputtering, saying, "What the fuck?" Called Cooder a madman.

Stopping at his car door, Cooder pointed a finger back at him, the guy turning down the rap music. Getting in, Cooder rolled up to the pickup window, got out a ten, took the bag and his change from the pimple-head kid. Rolling out of there, half expecting a SWAT team to swoop down, sticking a half-wrapped bagel in his mouth, throwing the wrapper down, he pulled back onto Pemberton and turned south. Now where the fuck was Angel? One eye out for him, the other looking out for the cops. One hand on the wheel, the other tucking food into his mouth.

Turning east on the first side street, he looked past a line of parked cars, a couple of dumpsters in a laneway on the south side. Doing a sweep from one street to the next, back and forth, checking between industrial buildings, the auto repair joints and paint shops. Made the bagels disappear, thinking he was still hungry, and with no sign of Angel or the kid. Could chance another run through the drive-thru, but maybe the rap guy called the cops. Looking at the bags of money on the floor, thinking better of it.

Replaying their conversation, Cooder considered what the kid overheard before jumping out. Then he spotted Angel over by Kiwanis Park, the man walking toward the Expedition, shaking his head and getting in, saying, "The fuck did you go?" Checking both money bags were still there.

"I had to swing around."

Angel looked at the wrappers and McDonald's bag under his feet. "You found time to eat, huh?"

"Got caught in a drive-thru."

"Think to get me something?"

Cooder grinned, saying, "You let the kid outrun you, huh?"

"What'd you think, I was gonna go pedophiling after her? Had to put on a show. By the time I got to the corner, the kid was fuckin' gone."

"And heard everything we said, all the way from Richmond. Calling each other by name." Cooder rolled back out to Pemberton, his eyes going left and right, watching for the kid or the cops.

"Just two guys shooting the shit, plus who's the kid gonna tell?" Angel waved it off. "Ten to one it's a runaway."

"How about she says you touched her?"

"Whoa, whoa. First off, that kind of thing doesn't fit my profile."

"Says the guy who ran after her."

"Last place a runaway goes is the cops."

"Okay, forget it. Let's go count it."

"First thing, we drop it off, then ditch the ride, just in case." Angel taking out his smokes, offering Cooder one, pressing in the lighter. "Fucking smell in here's got my stomach rolling."

« « «

Felt pretty good. A hundred and ten grand richer, all in a morning's work, the cash stashed behind a mound of pink insulation in Angel's attic, top of his closet. They drove to the Auto Mall, needing to dump the Expedition. Angel going in the body shop, coming back saying his guy wasn't in. Called him on his cell, was told to come back mid-afternoon. So they drove the couple of blocks to the dog park along the water, had another look around for the kid. Neither of them liking the idea of driving around this long in a stolen ride, agreeing to get something to eat before trying to drop it off again. Cooder driving back toward Mickey D's, the place done serving breakfast now. Passing a side street, he remembered the name of this place and swung into the Potlatch lot. The sign declaring it open.

"The fuck you doing?"

Cooder drove past its side entrance — the carved name and totems flanking the door — rolling to the gravel lot around back. One car and an RV parked there. Nobody going to spot the Expedition. Saying, "I knew this guy at Kent..."

"Paying on your two-year mistake."

Cooder gave him a look. Sorry he ever told him about the criminal assault charges after decking a player on the ice. Got a game misconduct for dropping the gloves, taking out the opposing forward. The guy took it personal and waited in the arena parking lot, Cooder finishing what they started on the ice, putting the guy in a coma. Claimed self-defense, the guy ambushing him, but ended up being charged with criminal assault. Second time he'd been charged with causing bodily harm, getting off with a year of community service the first time, the judge taking a dim view of a hockey goon taking it off the ice, decreeing he hadn't got the message, going maximum that second time.

Cooder saying, "A councillor called the Chief, a guy helping inmates on release back to the world, said this was the place."

"Place for what?" Angel looked around and pointed for him to park along the back of the building.

"The Chief's from around here — even said he'd seen me play, felt I got a bum deal. The two of us got to talking in the yard over hoops, the man getting me to walk a straight path, same time helping me with my jump shot. Told me I was a natural."

"Straight path, huh?"

"One time, we got to talking about food they weren't serving in Kent, the Chief telling me about this place, how they hang their meat, bake their buns fresh, their own home-made toppings. Man, all I could think about after."

"You want to go in and eat or put me to sleep?"

"Man practically had me tasting this place. Come on, get set for the best burger of your life." Cooder getting out.

"Really seeing why your woman slapped you." Angel opened his door.

"We eat, then go dump the ride." Cooder shutting his

door, smelling barbecue coming from a vent in back of the place, his mouth watering. Using the transmitter to lock the doors, he went past the totem pole, a carving above the entry.

Angel followed, letting his eyes adjust to the dim in the place, just a lone couple at the table by the door. Too early for the lunch crowd, which was alright with him.

Cooder swung onto a stool at the counter. Angel sat next to him, nodded to the withered-looking waitress. Saying yeah to a coffee.

The name tag made her to be Dell. Graying hair and a body bagged by a hard life. Setting oversized cups down, she fetched and handed each a menu, letting them know meatloaf was the day's special. Getting the coffee pot and pouring.

Cooder said to her, "Guy I know told me about this place. Maybe you know him, goes by the Chief?"

She didn't know anybody going by that.

"Said your burgers are the best around."

"Well, he's the Chief, right?" She smiled, saying, "You ask me, he steered you right, the best this side of the bridge anyway."

Angel scanned the menu, over a dozen burger choices, any way you like, assorted sandwiches, meatloaf or patty melt, all came with fries or rings, your choice.

Cooder went with the Honcho: beef, bacon, cheese, a grilled wiener, onion, mushrooms, lettuce, special sauce and a free-run egg on top. Told Dell to load on the works. "The onions, you brown 'em up?"

"Caramelized? Yup, sure do."

"I'll go with that, and the fries." Rubbing his palms together, not acting like a man who just had breakfast an hour back.

"You betcha." Dell looked to Angel, ready with her stub of pencil and yellow pad.

His eyes darting around the place, acting like he might get jumped. Pouring sugar in his cup, Angel went with the Original with smoked cheddar. "No onions and hold that egg." Saying he wasn't ready to see yolk running down the side.

"You can let his egg run up on mine. And give him rings, we'll share 'em." Cooder slurped coffee, the brew beating the hell out of the one at the casino.

Telling them the Original didn't get an egg, Dell pulled the order off her pad and stuck it on a pin by the pass window. Went and sat on a stool in the corner and let her dogs rest.

After a minute, they heard the patties slapped down on a hot grill, sizzling away. God, it smelled good in here.

Sipping his coffee, Angel turned to the entrance. The couple at a table were figuring how big a tip to leave, getting set to go.

Cooder leaned to Angel, saying, "You got enough to cover this, right?"

... *slinking*

Wren grew up in a small post-war place back in Steel Town. A brick bungalow like every other place on the block. Her dad worked the floor at Bargain Harold's till the company sold to Kresge's. Her dad promoted to manager over at University Plaza. Things were looking up the day he came home with the news and a new bike under his arm, promising her mother could quit her admin job at Stelco. They'd gone to dinner that night, celebrating. Her dad talking about a rancher for sale, on acreage on the escarpment, and everything was good with her world.

It had been a counter girl at Kresge's, half her dad's age from what her mom told her. Called it his filthy fling, a thing that led to the endless fights. Calling him a dirty bastard. Her dad moving into the guest room one week, then out of the house the next. Never called to talk to Wren, explain things to her. Something Wren had trouble understanding, at first thinking she did something wrong, like being too needy.

A month of reticence before her mom took the slide, going from doting to doping. Pill bottles of Percocet in the medicine cabinet, leading to mood swings and throwing up. Her mom going from doctor to doctor, finally forging prescriptions, leading to her arrest. When Stelco put her on leave, the slide to part-salary made short work of their savings, leaving a rising stack of unpaid bills on the kitchen table. Her mom staying out late, sometimes coming back the next morning, smelling like last night. Dope-sick and needing help, she talked about getting herself into detox. Blaming the dirty bastard.

Wren juggled homework with after-school shopping and keeping the house as mother and daughter switched roles. Wren caring for her shaking mom, coaxing her to eat, pulling a blanket around her when she fell asleep on the couch. Her mom telling her she was sorry. "Baby, you deserve more than this, the dirty bastard."

It went like that through the second term, her first year of high school, Wren keeping her grades and juggling their lives, then her mother was gone. Just didn't come home.

It could have been a snooping neighbor or maybe the homeroom teacher who called Child Services. Wren arriving late for school in yesterday's clothes too many times, falling asleep on her elbow in class, her grades starting to tumble. Getting called into the principal's office. Mr. Stone sat behind his desk, a big woman named Hendricks from Child Services filling the chair across from him. Sitting in the only other chair — like the hot seat — Wren lied all she could to this case worker, in her mind dubbing her Prune Woman.

Acting like she'd heard it all before, the Prune asked awful questions about her mother and father. About the fights, staying out nights, calling it neglect and abandonment. Coming by the house after that, wanting to speak to a mom who wasn't there, trying to locate her father, prying into Wren's home life. Wren acting like nothing was wrong, saying, "You just missed her," or "She had a meeting." Finally saying she wasn't a kid anymore. Ended up demanding to see a lawyer.

It was the only time the Prune smiled, saying, "Believe me, dear, we're on the same side here."

Doubting the hell out of it, Wren folded her arms and wanted to run out of there, away from her own house. But run where?

"You get to legal age, dear, you can get all the lawyers you want, but for now you're a minor, and your well-being's my job."

"It matter how I feel about it?"

"As soon as you reach legal age, dear, you can feel all you want. Till then, how about you give me a break. At my age, migraines are nasty business."

Wren pointed at her, told her she was tormenting a minor, then said, "How about I go live with my dad?"

"If you have a number, an address, some way to get in touch . . ." The Prune Woman giving her that poker look.

Wren searched for a smug comment, but knew this woman had heard it all.

The Prune sighed, saying, "We don't choose our parents, none of us."

The court order followed, the Prune Woman getting her way, coming back to the house with an associate, telling Wren to gather some belongings. The Prune quick for a big woman, jamming a foot to keep the door from slamming, the two women barging in, and after the arguing and Wren crying at the table of piled-up bills, she tried to bolt past them. Caught by the arm, she was removed from her home and put in the back of their car. Processed and placed in a youth home.

"It's a good, safe place," the Prune assured her.

Wren calling it lockdown. Six other kids she called inmates, two to a room, all on bunk beds, all waiting on foster placement.

The Prune came back a couple of days later, along with her clipboard, and held it like a shield out in front of her, doing a follow-up. Asking about Wren's adjustment.

"The place is a dump, and the food's lousy." Wren folded her skinny arms in front of her, didn't hide her dislike of the woman.

The Prune sat with her in the front room, scribbling on her pad, finally told her her mom had turned up and volunteered herself into rehab, determined to get cleaned up. Saying it was a positive step, commending her mom for trying. Talked for a while, then set the clipboard down and put a gentle arm around Wren, saying, "This is the tough part, baby, but you and me will get through it, your mom too."

"Sound like you're so sure," Wren said, not pulling away for a change, looking up at her, kind of hopeful and forcing herself not to cry.

"You can if you want?" the Prune said.

"Want what?"

"Cry."

Said she wasn't a kid anymore, but Wren stopped thinking of her as the Prune Woman after that.

"Can guess how you feel about this place, maybe about me too, and I can't blame you, not a bit, but believe me, you'll get through it."

"You keep saying that."

Miss Hendricks promised to arrange a phone call with her mom in the next couple of days. And asked if there was anything she could bring her.

"Mars bar." It was all she could think of, Wren testing her with a little thing. Hoping her mom made good on her end, the two of them getting through this awful time. Wren just wanting her life back the way it was.

Next time she came, Miss Hendricks placed the call from the front room, handing Wren her cell phone and a Mars bar, leaving her and closing the door behind her. Her mom coming on the line, asking, "How's my baby?" The two of them crying and talking. Her mom promising to beat this thing and be there for Wren.

And every time Miss Hendricks came, Mars bar in hand, Wren got her mom on the line. Her mom sounding better and better, finally seeking a court date, aiming to convince a judge she was getting her life back together. Asking for custody, and giving Wren new hope.

A few visits later, Wren could see something was wrong as soon as Miss Hendricks came through the front door. Asking Wren to sit down and explaining her mom got in front of the judge and made the appeal, but the courts got Wren's father mixed in, hearing testimony that her mother had been neglectful, unfit and addicted, the man citing incidents and offering proof. Claimed it was why he left. Had a couple of neighbors weigh in, supporting his position.

"What incidents, what proof, what neighbors?" Wren asked.

Hendricks read some of a sworn statement, one of the neighbors claiming Wren's mom had stumbled into her house one night, thinking she was in her own home. Same neighbor said her mom backed her car into her trash cans more than once. The couple to the rear yard had found her passed out by their clothesline and had to call the paramedics.

Wren made a fist, squishing the candy. Feeling hostile toward her dud dad, the man just getting back at her mom. Never called her, never asked about her. "Even drugs beats nothing."

Miss Hendricks said her father wasn't asking for child custody at this time. The court asking about Wren going to live with him and his new fiancée in Burlington. Said he applied for child support, showed that he couldn't do it financially on account of his new job, and his dependent fiancée.

Wren thinking he wanted nothing to do with her and his old life. Her hands in fists, Mars bar squishing between her fingers.

Miss Hendricks went and spoke with the judge, and next time she came, she sat Wren down in the front room, making a face like she just stepped in dog doo.

"He backed out, right?" Didn't matter to Wren, she'd given up on him by then.

"Told the judge it's a hard time right now, showed bank statements, a letter of projected income from his employer. His new job selling cars on commission is barely enough to scrape by."

"So I'm just his inconvenient kid."

"Said he's hoping down the road, three months maybe, but right now . . ."

"What road's that, the one paved with good intention?" Wren picked up a pillow off the armchair and punched it. "Got a nerve calling my mom unfit."

Miss Hendricks squeezed her shoulder, empathizing and saying, "Afraid that's not all . . ."

Wren looked at her. Pulling away and bracing herself.

"It's your mom."

And Wren couldn't speak, just looked at the woman.

"Got up from group therapy and left without a word."

"Left where?"

"We went to the house, but no sign she'd been back. The landlord changed the locks, on account of the rent. He put your stuff in the loft over the garage, willing to keep it for a month or two, but he wants the back rent and a cleaning fee."

Wren was out of her chair, her voice loud, "I was taking care of her, doing the housework, the cooking. Going to school. You came along 'helping,' and she's back on the street."

"We don't know, Wren. Look, addiction's not something —"

"Quit talking like I'm a dumb kid, okay?" Wren glared at her.

Miss Hendricks nodded.

Wren going to the window, looking out and trying to stop the tears. Miss Hendricks got up and put a hand on her shoulder. Wren drawing away, not wanting to be touched. All these adults towering over her and meaning well.

"I don't think you're a dumb kid. Far from it." Hendricks's eyes watered too, and she said, "My job's to see there's a roof over your head; God knows I want it to be the right one. A place where you can get back to school, be with friends, be a kid . . ."

"I had all that, school, friends, my home . . . then you showed up."

"It needs some time." The hurt showing in Hendricks's eyes.

"Meantime I just give up on my mom, right?"

"It's not you who gave up, Wren." In spite of the tough shell, the woman was crying, reaching in her purse for a pack of Kleenex.

Unclenching a fist, Wren took a tissue, wiping her eyes, then tooting her nose. Holding out her hand for another tissue, wiping chocolate off her fingers.

"I'm hoping your mom can turn it around, baby."

"You believe that?"

"I believe she wants to."

Wren bit her lip, wanted to call her Prune Woman. Could be she had her pegged right from the start. Right then, wanting to hurt her, the big dumb prune. But under the anger, Wren knew it wasn't her fault, just a civil servant doing her job, the best way she knew.

« « «

The days at the youth home crawled, with no more word from her mom, Wren asking whoever was on the front desk. Miss Hendricks came around less often to see her, until the time she came to say she'd found placement in foster care, trying to make it sound like good news, answering the same old question from Wren, having no further word from her mom.

A month and a half since she'd been taken from her home, Hendricks had her placed with the Nelsons, a nice couple with two young kids and a Newfie dog. Wren getting the pink room downstairs, a bathroom all to herself. It was the sneezing that turned out to be a red-eyed allergic reaction to the family pet. A hundred pounds of drooling dog named Bailey, an immovable lump on the family-room sofa, its airborne fur the most active thing about it. The fur getting into the vents and blown through the house. Had Wren itching her eyes and sneezing, which had the Nelsons concerned, calling the family doctor, and finally calling in Miss Hendricks.

Back at the youth home for a week before Hendricks came by and sat her down and held Wren's hand, giving her the saddest news. An overdose had taken her mom. Some hiker had found her in a park.

Hendricks in black, stood with Wren at the service, friends, neighbors and parents from school coming up and telling her how sorry they were. Her father showed up, hugged her and said he was so sorry. "Don't be mad at your mom, kiddo."

"I was never mad at her. It's you."

"You don't mean that."

She just looked at him and said, "So when am I coming to live with you?"

"Yeah, it's about this new job. A real son of a gun." Her dad looked at Hendricks for some support, got none, then looked back to Wren, said it would be soon. Then told her to hang in there.

Wren turned from him and walked away. Hendricks stepped up and leaned close to him, said something that made him wince, then followed the girl.

« « «

After the Nelsons, she landed with the Snows, a middle-age couple, Kevin and Donna. No giant dog, no kids of their own, but a couple of foster kids near her own age sharing an upstairs room, Robin and Maggie, a year apart, thirteen and fourteen, the picture of acne and awkward, both of them shy kids.

Sitting on the edge of the Murphy bed, Wren held the copy of *Unfu*k Yourself*. If Kevin Snow tried to enter, she'd hit him with it and run out of there.

He came and tapped on the door, saying "Nighty night," and she heard him go up the stairs. Then nothing but the sound of the clunking Frigidaire. She slept about two hours that night.

Miss Hendricks had excused her from school, set up a meeting with a councillor the following week, to help her process the loss of her mom. But Wren didn't want to talk.

Wasn't going to sit around blubbering, getting nowhere. And no way she wanted to hang around the Snows' house, opting to be in school instead. Unable to focus in class, her mind wandered from algebra and grammar to thinking about her mom, and how Kevin Snow had stood on the other side of her door, saying, "Nighty night." Knowing what he had on his mind.

Missed the school bus on purpose after class, took her time walking back to the house, considered telling Miss Hendricks about the creep. Thinking the old-prune side of the woman might have her seeing Wren as always causing problems. And what had the man done, seen her in her undies? The man sitting in his own kitchen, middle of the night, having a nightcap. No crime in that.

She kept to her room, missing TV and the chats with the other two girls. Telling Kevin Snow's wife Donna she had studies, excusing herself after supper. The other girls, Robin and Maggie, shared a room upstairs across the hall from the Snows', Wren hoping the door had a lock.

She read the way Kevin smiled at her anytime Donna wasn't watching. Maybe Donna knew but just couldn't deal with it. Kevin brushing by Wren when they passed in the hall. And doing little things like asking Wren to pass the veg and making contact with her hand, giving her shoulder a pat when she dried the supper dishes, bumping her hip, saying, "That a girl." Wren letting him know about boundaries by slapping his assuring hand, calling him Mr. Touchy Creepy.

Donna Snow seemed clueless, with her nobody-home eyes. Something Wren was too familiar with, that pill-glassy look with the dark circles and the down-the-street gaze. The woman working from home, making up gift baskets for a couple of local realtors.

Kevin kept up with his hands-on idea on foster parenting, touching the three girls whenever he got the chance. Doing it like it was friendly, making them feel right at home.

Donna withdrew to the backyard anytime the daylight and weather allowed, going through the mudroom and kneeling in her tiny garden plot and turning the soil, pulling weeds and stones, maybe pretending her life wasn't rotten — same as Wren's mother had done — Donna's fingers digging the soil, getting it under her nails.

Before breakfast the second-to-last morning, Wren came in the kitchen for some OJ, catching Kevin kneeling up on the counter, his bum crack showing like a hairy line above his belt loops, his dirty-soled white socks, and a cookie tin in his hand. Turning, he asked, "What the hell now, girl? You're supposed to be sleeping." Nothing friendly, holding the cookie tin close like it was an infant in need of hiding.

Acting sleepy with a yawn, Wren said her throat was scratchy, just wanted some juice. Kevin telling her breakfast was in a half hour. Stopping past the fridge, Wren listened and heard him replacing the tin, guessing it was at the back of the top shelf. Going to the den, quietly closing the door, she heard him thud down off the counter, then tread back up the stairs.

Didn't see him again until supper, the man all friendly then, talking about his day at the plant, asking about everybody else's day. Listening like he cared.

When the dishes were cleared, he came from behind Wren as she helped herself to a coffee from the carafe, planning to take it to her room. Kevin standing too close behind her, saying, "Well, look who's all grown up."

Bringing the cup around, she spilled some down his shirt front, saying, "*Oopsie.*"

Jumping back, he swiped at himself. Angry, saying, "That's what you got to say, *oopsie?*"

"Guess I'm at that awkward stage." She shrugged, took a sip, saying, "Good and hot, though, the way I like it."

Glancing around, seeing that Donna was out of earshot, he said, "Might want to remember whose house you're in, kiddo." Going to the paper towel dispenser under the cabinet. Then he went for the stairs, changed his shirt before he had to explain it to the wife. Stopping at the banister, he looked back, saying, "One call from me, and you're back in shelter hell."

"Yeah, but one call from me . . ." Wren letting it hang, sipping her coffee, watching him go up, thinking Child Services should've told him she was allergic to mutts. Going to the den, she closed the door. Knowing he wouldn't leave it there. Looking for some way to jam the door. Couldn't get the chair to wedge under the knob. She found a box of thumbtacks in the top drawer, counted out two dozen and placed them points-up on the carpet at the threshold.

Next morning, she gathered them up, and after a bowl of Frosted Flakes, she thanked Donna for the baloney and apple lunch, slipped the paper bag in her backpack and laced up her sneakers. Kevin coming into the front hall, smiling, saying he was sorry about catching her in her undies, and the spilled coffee, blaming the mishaps for the two of them getting off on the wrong foot. And he offered out his hand.

She looked at it, saying it wasn't his foot she was concerned about. Maybe she shouldn't have said it with Donna back in the kitchen. Leaving his hand hanging, she tried to move past him for the door. "You want to move or you want to write me a note? I'm going to be late for class."

He lowered his hand, then said, "The other girls are fine, settled right in. How d'you explain that?"

"How do you explain teeth marks?" She smiled and waited till he shifted to the side, and she was out of there.

Letting go a long breath and striding down the walk. Pushing back the tears she felt coming, telling herself not to be such a little kid.

Knowing she should call Miss Hendricks from the school office, let her know how it was really going. Just not sure how the woman would take news like that. Wondered if she even knew what sex was, just didn't look the type. Plus, this being the second placement for Wren, it would likely land on her. And the other two girls were doing fine. Wren going down the sidewalk, hurrying to catch the school bus.

« « «

Didn't take in much science in first class, then did some sketching in art, her heart not in it, followed by history about Upper and Lower Canada, then came that welcomed bell. She sat on her own at lunch and spent gym class thinking about not going back to that house. Just had nowhere else to go.

Borrowed a smoke from one of the grade eights after last class, struck a match when she got off school grounds, skipped the yellow bus and walked the dozen blocks, decided not to call Miss Hendricks. Thing was, if the other girls didn't have a problem, then doubting eyes would turn to Wren. Careful what you ask for, her mother would say. Or the one about going from the pot to the fire, another one of her mom's faves. Feeling queasy from the tobacco, Wren sucked a Tic Tac and finally went up to the house, stepping inside as it was getting dark. Told Donna she signed up for handball and had an after-school practice.

Supper was Habitant soup, toast scraped with butter and chocolate pudding. Not much talk going around the table that evening. Kevin Snow in a funk, brooding about something that happened at the packing plant. Never even looked at her.

Outside of "How was your day, dear?" Donna dished up the bowls and sat bleary-eyed and quiet, rosy-cheeked from working her garden. Robin and Maggie giggled about some cute boy in their class. Robin giving him an eight, Maggie handing out a seven on account of the braces, wondering what it would be like to kiss someone with tin teeth, maybe with spinach stuck in between. Both girls going, "*Eww.*" Then reevaluating their scores. Sitting next to each other, Wren guessing they were bumping feet, like some morse code language all their own. Wren saying she thought she knew the boy they meant — a grade behind her — and said, "Yeah, he's kinda cute."

Maggie asking for her score, Wren saying, "Seven. Eight when he loses the tin teeth." Building some rapport, the first time the other girls had said much to her since she moved in. Wren knowing that was on her, still bummed about losing her mom and keeping mostly to herself.

Before lights-out, Wren took care to be stealthy going up the creaky stairs, saw the light under the girls' door, heard the Snows down in the living room, the TV on. Slipping into their bedroom, she shut the door behind her, smiling at Robin and Maggie, both on their twin beds and on their phones, looking up as she came in. She started some small talk, first about school, then asked about forums they were into, music they liked — trying to open up to them — then got around to asking how they liked it here.

Both girls shrugged, saying it was alright, a look passing between them. Wren cut to it, replaying the night she went to the powder room in her undies, how Kevin turned on the light and stared at her. Told some of what came after, setting him out to be a total creep. Wanting to know their thoughts. Got nothing from Robin. Maggie asking why she walked around in her undies in the first place, then saying Donna was nice.

"Donna's nice, yeah, but like the living dead. In her own world most of the time, or just looking the other way." Wren making it plain, saying Kevin was a total perv. How they all ought to cut out of there, at least report him. Put her middle finger over her index, saying her and Miss Hendricks were like this. Said she'd make the call, if they backed her up.

"You're just gonna get everybody mad," Robin said.

"Can get as mad as they want. The man's still a perv."

Maggie said she didn't know what she meant by that, so Wren replayed the scenes with Kevin getting touchy-feely, blocking her from leaving that very morning. "Seen him touch you too. So don't say you don't know."

"It's just him being friendly, being a father figure. We just take off, leave this roof over our heads?" Robin glanced up. "Warm beds, packed lunch every day, supper when we get home. And the school's not too bad." Robin shook her head. "You got something like that out there?"

"Not sure you see what's coming."

"What I see, Kevin's just like that, maybe just being friendly."

"He's a creep, in capital letters." Wren careful to keep her voice down. "Come on, you'd have to be blind . . ."

"Donna's not going to let anything happen," Maggie said, crossing her arms and repeating, "She's nice."

"Making soup and bagging your lunch, that's not going to do it."

"Let me ask again, you got something like that out there, a warm blanket and a hot meal?" Robin said. "We listen to you, and we'll be scrounging around in a dumpster."

"You're going to be a victim, that's what, you hang around here." Looking from Robin to Maggie. Maggie with the fear in her doe eyes. Wren seeing she wasn't getting anywhere.

"The three of us take off," said Robin, "it's going to end up a whole lot worse, out there on our own. Any idea what wants to touch you out there?"

"Why I'll call Hendricks. The three of us stepping up together and saying how it is."

Putting her phone on the bed, Maggie tugged her knees up, hugged a pillow, burying her face into it.

"Happy now?" Robin said.

Coming at it another way, Wren said, "Come on, a robin and a wren. And Maggie, you be the magpie. The three of us'll fly out of here, you'll see." Maggie in fear, Robin in denial, Wren seeing it was no use. Telling them to forget it, she eased open the door, heard Kevin's voice from the living room, then tiptoed down in the dark, back to the den.

That night was a long one of lying on the pull-out, the thumbtacks like teeth in front of the door. She tried as hard as she could, tried to connect with her mom, wanting to know what to do, but getting nothing. Halfway through the night, she set her mind; she was going, no idea where, just knew she was getting out of there. She'd call Miss Hendricks and tell her side of it, knowing Kevin would have his own version. If nothing else, maybe the call would get him to lay off the other girls. Knowing Miss Hendricks would be keeping watch.

Wren found some sleep in the pre-dawn, but then she felt Kevin Snow's weight and breath on her neck. Those feral eyes. Those hands pressing her down so she couldn't breathe. Jumping up in the bed, gasping in air, her whole body in sweat, the nightmare taking too long to fade, her heart pounding out of her throat.

Didn't dare sleep after that, afraid that dream would come again. Not sure the tacks and the hardcover book were enough. She sat against the wall, the pillow at her back, and she watched out the window, the dark of the cinder blocks next door. Did it until the dark gave way to the morning gray. Folding up the bed when she heard movement from upstairs, Wren crouched and picked up the thumbtacks and put them back in the tray in the desk.

By seven thirty, Donna Snow was clinking around in the kitchen, putting on a pot, setting out the milk and Kellogg's, fixing Kevin some eggs, waiting while he laced up his work boots, pecked his cheek and handed him the sack lunch, seeing him off for his meat-packing job. Smiling as she hustled the three girls off to school, passing out more lunch bags. Wren guessed Donna had been popping, looked like she was in that zone, Wren too familiar with the signs.

Thanking Donna as she went out the door, betting the woman would sit at the table with her coffee and glazed eyes. Staring out, maybe trying to focus on putting in next spring's tulip bulbs.

Letting the two girls get ahead on the way to the school bus, neither turning or waiting for her. Wren cut down a side street, going in a different direction, lingering at a four-way, like she was waiting on a ride, almost wishing she had another smoke, knowing it would flip her stomach again.

Yeah, she ought to call Miss Hendricks, and then something popped into her mind. The sight of Kevin Snow up on the kitchen counter. Surprised she hadn't thought of it before. And she turned around, retracing her steps, a scheme taking shape by the time she saw the roof of the Snows' house, and like that, she knew what to do. From the corner, she could see Donna in the front window, sitting at the breakfast table, staring out at nothing, holding a cup in both hands.

Out of sight behind a cedar, Wren waited till Donna was gone from the window. Giving it a few more minutes, she crossed the street and walked up the drive, hoping the front door wasn't locked, getting ready with some line about forgetting her math notes. She slipped into the house and listened, hearing nothing but the fridge. Tiptoeing down the hall to the mudroom, she looked out, seeing Donna in the backyard, assessing her garden plot.

Wren went and hoisted herself onto the kitchen counter, reached in back of the cereal cupboard, taking out the cookie tin. Popping the lid, she fished inside and took the banded cash from the tin — the money Kevin had tucked in there.

Shoving it in a pocket, she checked the mudroom window again, Donna on her knees digging. Going upstairs, Wren nicked some basic cosmetics from the woman's bathroom cabinet. Feeling bad for taking what she guessed was the rainy-day cash, feeling worse for Donna, stuck with a man like that and not seeing a better way for herself.

Then she was out of there and going in the opposite direction. Still feeling the nerves at the bus shelter, applying lipstick, trying to see her reflection in the shelter's glass, finally taking the rolled bills and counting off nearly seven hundred, organizing them into fifties, twenties and tens. More than she'd ever seen at one time, and more than enough for a one-way fare to the far coast. According to the web page: four hundred and forty-four bucks plus tax on Via Rail. Didn't know a soul out there, but what did she have here? No point looking up her dud dad, knock on his door and say, "Hey ya, Daddy. You miss me yet?"

Careful not to go Tammy Faye with the make-up, what her mom would call it, first time in her life Wren spread on the lipstick, felt weird having it on her mouth. Brushing some eyeliner and blush, tacking a few years to her looks.

Not much she could do with her hair. Telling herself age was mostly about attitude.

Asking the 512 bus driver for directions, she sat in the front seat, riding to the Oakville GO station, the uniformed attendant telling her to catch the train to Toronto, right to Union Station. Checking her ID and selling her a one-way ticket to the West Coast.

. . . *fade to black*

Didn't linger on the thought. Fitch having a good idea of the kind of fit Annie would pitch. Putting his piece in his mouth or under his chin and winning the battle with cancer. Shaking hands with Elvis wasn't much of a win, just a quicker way out. But it wasn't in his nature. Top of that Annie would be standing by those gates, her arms crossed and her mouth set tight, glaring at him as he crossed over. And there'd be hell to pay, even in heaven.

He would face the cancer straight on. Right then, he was taking in the view of the inlet, glancing at his watch, seeing how long before the Potlatch opened, looking forward to meatloaf.

Then there they were again, the same two men, coming the other way, still looking tense. Fitch couldn't hear the words, just the harsh tones. His eyes on them.

The smaller one glanced over, holding his gaze as they passed, saying, "I help you with something, old buddy?"

Fitch didn't answer, just kept looking at them, sitting in his lounge out front of the Winnebago, sizing them up like he was still on the job.

"Get a load of this guy," the smaller one said, the other one saying he was likely deaf, taking his pal by the sleeve, moving them along, going past Fitch.

The smaller one shaking his head, laughing it off, saying something about lost marbles.

. . . *riding the rails*

L ooking at herself in the mirror, standing in the GO
station's washroom, Wren was thinking the lipstick
could use a re-coat, seeing she missed some of her mouth.
Not sure whether to wipe off the old or just touch it up. Had
always been more of a lip balm girl, going with Burt's Bees
watermelon.

Catching the late-afternoon GO train. Wren acted like
she was no stranger to travel, her backpack over a shoulder,
no need of a parent or guardian. Walking through Union
Station like she owned the place. Showing the man in the
cap the one-way rail pass to Vancouver, telling him she'd like
a window seat.

The man asking, "You with somebody, miss?"

"I get that a lot." Smiling the painted mouth and reaching
in a pocket, Wren showed the ticket agent the same ID she
showed the uniformed guy in Oakville. The ID she bought
back at her old school in Hamilton, back when she was living
with her mom. Her school buddy Tia getting the bright idea
after googling some site offering real IDs — no questions
asked, the only requirement was cash up front. Some of the

lunch crowd got in on it, pooling allowances, fifty bucks each after the group discount, Tia arranging the money transfer under one of her mom's accounts. Two weeks later a plain-wrapped package showed up in a rented UPS box, the IDs inside the pages of a couple of foreign romance novels. Discarding the paperbacks, the girls all walked away, going from Barbies to bar drinks, just like that.

The ticket agent handed back her ID and the pass, telling Wren to enjoy the trip. Finding out the station closed before one in the morning, she caught the express bus to the airport, walking through the bustle, sitting in domestic arrivals, moving from gate to gate, then on to departures. Spending time in washroom cubicles. Finally walking to international arrivals, letting the evening turn to night and back to early morning, bored out of her mind. Walking from the terminal before security started asking questions, she took the early bus to Kipling Station, the subway taking her back to Union Station. Wren sitting in the food court, having coffee and a muffin, waiting on her train, the Canadian, set to pull out at quarter to ten.

After boarding, she curled on the window seat in coach, her backpack on the floor by her feet. One parent gone, and the other not wanting her, she was set to let the rails rock her for three days and four nights, taking her to a new life, the Canadian hooking past Sudbury and Sioux Lookout, the top of the Great Sea, across the tabletop patchwork of the prairies, through the Rockies and on to the coast.

Riding through central Ontario, Wren looked out at the farmers on their red and green machines, getting in their harvest. Nobody sat next to her on the first leg, and she was grateful for it, stretching out across both seats. When evening fell they were passing someplace called Capreol. Tried to sleep going past Foleyet and Elsas, and was still awake as they made the stop in Hornepayne. Stepping out on the platform in the middle of nothing, she stretched her legs and bummed a smoke off some bearded guy with watering eyes, puffed and felt the cold biting at her. Again, she asked herself why she was smoking. Okay, it made her appear older, but it was flipping her stomach something awful. And it was habit-forming, and who needed that? She stubbed it out, telling herself never again.

Back up the car's metal stairs, she made another try for sleep, and in spite of the gentle rocking, she was staring out at the night, the miles rumbling past till the Canadian stopped again, yielding to a freight that took priority on the rails. Still tasting the stale tobacco, she walked between the rows of dozing riders, a few heads hanging into the aisle, Wren going from one car to the next, sitting at a table under the dome of the skyliner, the car empty but for the guy she'd bummed the smoke from, stretched and sleeping at the far end, his hoodie up over his head. Just the beard showing.

Getting underway again, the Canadian chugged — Wren stared out at the moon over miles of open land, the night full of stars. The car door opened and an elderly woman stepped from the forward car passing the sleeping man. Coming to the rear, she looked around, smiled and asked if Wren could do with some company.

Wren shrugged and said, "Sure."

Her name was Maude — about Wren's height, strands of gray streaking her brunette hair, coifed in a short bob. A leather handbag and a sweater hooked on her arm, a polished look about her. Sitting opposite, she set down a Margaret Atwood novel, and offered her free hand over the table, crinkled like an old leaf with a sparkling ring on her finger. Saying, "Supposed to be relaxing, but for the life of me, I can't catch a wink."

94

"Yeah, same here." Wren smiled, shook her hand, saying her name, then, "My first time on the rails."

"Me too." Maude nodded and looked out. "Any idea where we are, Wren?"

"Just someplace, the middle of the night." Wren shrugged and smiled. "Conductor said we'll make Winnipeg around eight, about a half hour late."

"You visiting relations?" Maude asked.

Told the woman she was going to see her father in Vancouver, how it had been too long. Told her every time he saw her he made such a fuss, going on about how much she'd grown, and always had a gift for her. Swallowing the golf ball in her throat, Wren threw in that he was in the movie biz, busy working on a picture.

"How exciting. At Lionsgate?"

"Think that's it."

"Oh my, and what does he do?"

"Think he's directing this one, a feature." Wren doing a lousy job of lying. Then asking about Maude.

Calling this her separation slog, Maude was hoping the silver rails would sort things out and help get her life on track.

"By slog you mean . . ."

"Divorce, dear. A terrible thing, but the shackles are off." Maude brightened. "Two nights of 'Pamper Me' at the Fairmont. Exfoliation, rejuvenation, massage, the works. Going to get my glow back, and start by getting up when I want. I might take the trolley through Stanley Park, see the belugas, or I could go shop Robson and Gastown, the kind of things my ex hated to do. Do it with nobody tagging along checking his watch. Get a fresh perspective, but I'm not sure you understand all that yet."

"Could've just tied him to the tracks," Wren said.

"Ah, you do understand." That brought a chuckle, Maude saying her own upbringing forbade that sort of thing. Wagging a finger, saying, "You're a real pistol, I can see we're going to get along."

"Yeah, that's another way to do it — a pistol."

Maude laughed, asking, "So how long you staying with your dad?"

"If I like it, I mean Vancouver, I might stay awhile." Wren mentioned he bought her a one-way, how it was up to her. Said she wouldn't mind the nicer weather.

Maude nodded, looked like she had more questions, but didn't ask any. And they both stared out at the moon.

Wren finally saying, "Funny, how life's bigger in the dark."

"I think I know what you mean, dear. Me, I just cleared my board of a hundred and fifty pounds of lord and master. Only thing that'll keep me up from here on is coffee and garlic." Maude smiled again, saying, "Oh, that reminds me, I don't know if you're peckish . . ." Reaching into her leather bag. "The server in the diner wrapped this for me. I just went for the cheesecake and a glass of pinot, but it seems the meal's included in the fare. Didn't want to hurt his feelings, so I took a doggie bag." Tapping her nose, saying, "Old snoot tells me it's got a touch of the bud, garlic, so I didn't chance it." Taking out a neatly wrapped tinfoil, Maude peeled back its edge, let Wren look at a nice fillet of salmon, a bed of rice pilaf on the side, some julienned cucumber, along with a lemon wedge. The salmon with the grill marks smelled fantastic. Maude getting out a tiny tub with some kind of dressing.

"Can only get tea or coffee till morning." Wren's mouth watered. Swallowing, saying Via only accepted credit card payments nowadays, and that she'd only brought cash, and how it had kept her from getting something to eat.

"Well, you'll be saving me from temptation then." Maude slid it forward, saying, "That is, if garlic's not your Achille's heel."

"No problem far as I know." Hadn't had a bite since the muffin, before that it was Frosted Flakes at the Snows'. Looking at it, being casual about it, saying, "Well, I'd sure hate to see it go to waste."

Maude nodded and fished a paper napkin wrapped around a plastic knife and fork. "Good, I abhor waste too."

"I mean, if you're really sure?"

"Never more so, dear."

Wren unfolded the tented foil wrap, realized how hungry she was. Taking the lemon wedge and squirting, cutting and spearing a bite of salmon, sawing an asparagus spear — it sure was good. Held back from wolfing it down and moaning, not wanting the poor manners of starvation to show. Dipped a sliver of cucumber in the honey-sweet dressing and popped it in her mouth. Had never given cukes a second thought until then. When she finished, she reached the napkin, thanking Maude again, said she didn't notice any garlic, and offered to pay for the meal.

"On the contrary, dear. You just saved me a measure of guilt."

"Well, glad I could help." Grinning, Wren wiped again with the napkin, getting up and tossing the tissue and foil in the trash, sitting back across from Maude. And it came with no warning, she was crying, no idea why she was wiping an eye with her sleeve, saying, "Got some lemon in my eye." A lame thing to say. She pulled it together and said the truth of it was her parents had split up after she'd been watching them fight ever since she could remember. Ended with her dad walking out, and moving out west. Wren somehow feeling it was her fault. Didn't want to talk about her mom dying, or her bouncing from youth homes to foster care, and sure didn't want to say why she ran away from Kevin Snow.

Maude reached a hand across and took hers, said she never should have brought up her own marital split, thinking it was the cause of Wren's tears, feeling just awful for it. Wren letting her hold her hand. Maude told her she never had any kids. "So I'm out of my depth here, dear, but we don't pick our parents, do we? And one thing I'm sure about, it's not your fault."

"Glad you didn't say it'll all work out in the end."

Maude patted her hand. "You're too clever for that."

And it turned into what her mom would have called a gabfest, lasting till the streaks of dawn showed someplace over Winnitoba. Wren talked of growing up near Steel Town, her friends, her school, sports she liked to play, keeping her troubles to herself. Maude saying how she had played doubles tennis for years, acting as mate on his sailboat, calling her ex old-what's-his-name. And how she needed to find some new things on her own.

Getting to know each other, filling the air, yet allowing the quiet spaces — Maude calling them two single gals riding the rails, destiny putting them together — comfortable in each other's company, insisting she take care of breakfast, croissants and fruit, warning Wren about the Via coffee. Wren going to the café on the lower level and getting cups of hot water in a tray, along with those little creamers, producing teabags she'd taken from the Snows' pantry when she stole the money. The two of them sitting under the dome, dunking Tetley bags in their styro cups, gaining an appreciation for riding the rails, the commonwealth blurring by, prairie green and harvest gold, here and there patches of snow.

When the steward came around, taking reservations for the dining car, Maude insisted there'd be two for lunch, admitting she needed to catch a nap before then, excusing herself to her cabin, what she called an oversized broom closet, asking if Wren minded. Wren saying she could use a cat nap herself, meeting her later in the dining car. Wren insisting on paying for her own meal, showing she had cash. Maude not hearing about it, saying it was the rule of the rails, grown-ups got to pay. "Plus Via doesn't take cash payment anymore, remember?" Saying what a delight Wren's company was, felt it was the least she could do.

The Canadian pulled into Pacific Central just past six on the fourth evening, full dark coming on. Maude said, "I know I already asked, but you sure you'll be okay?"

"I can take care of myself."

"Yes, I think we covered that."

"Guess we did, but my dad'll come get me."

"Except he's not expecting you. Think you said that too."

"On account it's a surprise."

"Right. Well, how about we share a cab? I'll have the cabbie drop you."

"Just going to call him, and he'll come pick me up, but thanks." Wren looked at Thornton Park in front of the station — drunken voices coming from a bench, the outline of someone rolled in a sleeping bag, a shopping buggy over-flowing with plastic bags — didn't need to be told this was the sketchy side of town. But Wren's wall was up, the one not letting anybody too close. And she sure didn't want her new friend seeing her as a nuisance, or an underaged runaway. A fugitive, in fact, after stealing the money from Kevin Snow's cookie tin.

Maude took out her phone and offered it to her.

"They got pay phones inside." Wren aimed a thumb behind her.

"Maybe one time they did, but this is the cellular age, dear. Not many pay phones to be found these days. Ones that are left are germ- and graffiti-ridden, likely to catch something." Smiling and still holding out her cell.

Wren nodded, took it and tapped in numbers, turned away and waited. Clicked off and handed it back, saying, "Went to voicemail. Guess I'll try later."

"Don't want to nag, dear, but I've got a room right at the Fairmont. You can try again from there."

Wren looked at the darkness of the park across from the station, hearing the voices. Getting hard to argue. Watching her frosty breath, Wren took a moment, then agreed.

Raising her hand, Maude signaled the lead cab in the line, the cabbie pulling forward, getting out to help with Maude's suitcase, Wren hanging onto her backpack, getting in back and sliding across, Maude getting in next to her, pulling the door shut, telling the cabbie where she wanted to go. Wren looking out, the shadows of two men getting into a fistfight out on Main.

. . . *not much on goodbyes*

Watching Wren hang up the phone in the suite, Maude said, "What say I have the front desk roll in a cot, and you get a good night's rest. You can try again in the morning." Holding up a hand before Wren could answer. Maude saying, "It's no trouble, and you know I'm happy for the company."

Maybe it was a dumb move, Wren not wanting to be more beholden to this kind woman than she already felt. And not much on goodbyes, Wren slept on the cot, then got up at first light and slid into her jeans, caught the strap of her backpack, slipped into her sneakers and went for the door. Whispered a goodbye, she eased it shut and got on the elevator.

No idea about this city, damper but warmer than back east. Downtown just coming to life in the morning. A city bus unloaded passengers, commuters getting off, others getting on.

Hunching in her hoodie, Wren turned into a café on West Georgia and joined the lineup at the counter. Ordered a large, then walked the city as the shadows shrank on the concrete between the buildings. Looking in shop windows, stopping for an early lunch at a pushcart and buying a brat with the works, she talked the vendor down to five bucks even. Walked toward the water and found a bench, shared some of the bun with a pigeon, six more showing up with their bobbing heads. Wren making sure each one got a fair share. Then she wandered some more, taking in the new city, not sure if it was going to be home, and no idea about her next move.

Running from the Snows, she had figured there would be plenty of time to sort things out on the train. Walking past the steam clock in Gastown, she spied a rolled blanket on a bench in a parkette. Nobody around it, and the blanket looked good enough, no stains or smells. Wren tucked it under an arm and walked back to West Georgia, nobody yelling, "Hey!" and chasing after her. She was walking toward Stanley Park.

Mid-afternoon, she stopped to listen to a skinny street musician, dreads and a beard, playing an acoustic at the corner of Denman and West Georgia, near the edge of the park with a nice glimpse of the water and the North Shore mountains. Strumming an old James Taylor number, "Steamroller." And the guy could sing. She dropped a quarter in his wool hat, and he thanked her, asking, "Where you from?"

"Makes you think I'm from somewhere?"

"The way you look at the peaks."

"How's that?"

"Like every tourist who hasn't seen them before."

Wren looked around at the veins of white showing at the top, asking what it was called, and he said that was Grouse.

"So, what do you like?" he asked, meaning a song.

"I don't know, that was pretty good."

And he played Springsteen's "The River." Then he told

her his set was designed for the usual tourist types that came by, songs that got the toes tapping and the fingers tipping. Being late in the season, the afternoon crowd had thinned on account of the cold, and he got up, told her it was hard to play when your fingers got numb, and he zipped the guitar in its case, pocketing the money from the hat, shifting a paper shopping bag under an arm, and shouldering the guitar by the strap. He said, "I'm Patch, by the way, and guessing by the roll, you're camping out, what I call roughing the rainforest."

"I'm not sure yet," she said.

"Well, I'm heading for supper, my off-the-grid griddle. And you're welcome to join us. And so you know, the us part is my girl and my dog."

She looked in the direction of the park, the way this rail of a guy was heading, saying, "You live through there?"

"Not through, but in." Smiling, Patch said, "Come on, see for yourself."

Wren followed along the path, palmed a good stone just in case, and listened to him talk over his shoulder, explaining he'd been looking for work, how jobs were in short supply, and busking was making ends meet.

Turned out the camp was off a trail fifty yards behind Lost Lagoon, in sight of the Jubilee Fountain, yet tucked under the pines. Home was a canvas tarp, with heavy plastic duct-taped or stitched to make its sides, a Hefty bag acting as the front door. Out front was a small clearing.

Dropping the stone when Patch introduced her to Jade, a sweetheart of a blonde, not much older than she was. Wren shook hands, feeling at ease right away, then was patting Luke, a mutt of shepherd and setter ancestry, forgetting she was allergic.

Dressed in fatigues, it turned out Jade was from a prairie town nobody ever heard of. A natural girl with a pretty face and blunt-cut hair. Her story was she didn't see eye to eye with her parents about her life choices, so she split.

Patch had been pink-slipped in the spring from his job at a marijuana farm in the Fraser Valley, too much sampling. And since his pay ran out, they ditched their two-room apartment in Mission, came out here, and he turned to corner music and pocket change. Patch mapped out different corners, playing his sets any day it wasn't raining. And Luke was left to guard Jade and the fort.

Jade insisted Wren stay for supper and the night, explaining it was risky out there, some of the homeless teetered on the edge, soundness of mind in short supply. That and Jade loved to have company over. Stirring a ladle in a blackened pot of mushroom and potato soup, cooking over a tiny camp stove, its propane tank hanging on the side. Turned out the soup was pretty good, Wren having a second helping, sitting on a ground sheet cross-legged, eating by lantern light. Patch rinsed and wiped the bowls, Jade putting water on for coffee.

When the dark came, Patch lowered the lantern flame, not wanting to draw attention, and they talked a while, then got into the shelter, Wren unrolling her blanket in a corner, opposite the couple, Luke settling in front of the plastic trash-bag door, putting his head on his paws.

Lying on half, she pulled the rest of the blanket over herself, used her backpack like a pillow, ignored the poking stones under the ground sheet, said goodnight and shivered herself to sleep, hearing their whispers and glad for their company. Once she woke with a start, seeing Kevin Snow's face against hers, the man's hands on her. Her heart hammered and she rubbed her hands together, cupped them and blew into them, part of her wanting to stumble out of there and find her way back to the Fairmont, ask the front desk to ring Maude's room. Knowing she wouldn't find her way out of the park at night. Lying there, she listened to Patch mumbling in his sleep, Jade *shh*ing, settling him. The dog snoring by the plastic-bag door. Wren getting a scratchy throat and her eyes burned, being allergic to Luke, but it wasn't too bad.

Lying awake and cold, thoughts of her mom and living back in their house came to her. Recalling details of her room, what it felt like to be there, the sights and smells, seemed so long ago. Afraid those memories might fade away. Funny, she never gave a thought to feeling safe or warm back before her world turned upside down.

At first light, Jade stirred and was up, boiling water for coffee, Wren helping out, making peanut butter and jelly sandwiches. After breakfast, she thanked them and rolled up her blanket. Patch said his last set would be at the same spot, the corner at Denman where they'd met, unless it was raining.

"You need a place to crash, you're welcome anytime," Jade told her, giving her a hug. Patch and Luke showed her the way along the narrow path, and she made her way out of the park, deciding to cross to the North Shore, walking past the stone statues and onto the Lions Gate, the bridge vibrating from all the cars, people heading into the city early. Standing at the arch, she felt the early sun on her face, a freighter passing under the bridge and into the harbor.

Took the path on the north side of the bridge and followed it around to a dog park and duck pond. Crossed a ball field and a single set of tracks, went past a gallery that had once been a ferry building. Sat on a log by the Seawall as the morning warmed, looking across at the city, past the park where she had slept. When the south mall of Park Royal opened, she got a Booster Juice at the food court, washed up and brushed her teeth in the public washroom. Made her way through Park Royal Village, past a fake lighthouse with a bar underneath, nabbed an apple at Whole Foods. Sent God a thought bubble, said she was sorry about the sin, but necessity was the mother of taking chances — another one of her mother's pearls. Wondering what Miss Hendricks would think about petty theft. Probably write *thief* on her clipboard and underline it.

But that was it for stealing. Getting caught meant she'd get processed and sent back to Child Services. Couldn't explain the money she stole, or justify that Kevin Snow had it coming. It started raining when she crossed Marine, and she went inside the north mall, walked through the Bay, hung around a trendy workout place, then window-shopped to stay dry. Going back to the south mall in the afternoon, she did the same thing, sitting on benches and looking in shop windows. Stayed warm and dry. Pretty sure a security guard had noticed and was dogging her. Wren seeing him walking behind her in the reflection of the Eddie Bauer window, the rolled-up blanket and backpack likely screamed homeless girl.

Going up the escalator, she ordered a Cold Cut Combo and an orange juice. Sitting at a table near some old men speaking a foreign language, she found a section of the *Globe* and took her time flipping its pages. The same security guy strolled by a couple of times, still glancing over. When the rain stopped hitting the skylights high above the food court, she tossed out her trash, put the tray on a rack, and wove through the mall, exiting at the Dollarama.

The afternoon warmed and she walked the trail along the Capilano, found a TransLink card and tucked it in a pocket. At the mouth of the river, she went west through the same dog park, past the duck pond with its willows hanging down around it, a mini-golf course on the opposite bank. Going along the ocean and napping behind a log on Ambleside

Beach, across from English Bay, she was warm and caught up on some sleep.

Showing the pass to a bus driver back on Marine, she took the double-zone ride, going back across the bridge and through the city, catching the SkyTrain into the YVR airport. Spent the evening shifting seats from one departure lounge to the next, people coming and going with their suitcases on wheels, nobody looking twice at a girl with a backpack and rolled blanket. At domestic arrivals, she made like she was waiting on somebody coming off a red-eye. Then over to an international departure gate, sitting till final boarding was called, then she went and stood in front of the arrival/departure board. Guessing security would eventually pick her up on their cameras, and come asking questions, maybe hold her for the cops. All of it ending with her being sent back to Miss Hendricks and that foster hell. She needed to come up with a plan.

Giving in to a ten-pack of Timbits, she asked the counter woman for the time — just past five in the morning — and she sat at the Tim's counter, organizing tiny donuts by the ones she'd eat first, biting into an apple fritter. Overhearing a middle-aged pair at the next table talking about the money the husband had pissed away at the Rock, the wife calling him a boob, giving him a dressing-down about losing their vacation money, just like everything else in his life. The man said no amount of nagging would bring it back, losing one jackpot and getting into another. Their words were heating, and Wren couldn't handle another griping couple, never wanted to hear it again in her whole life. Then seeing a security guard looking over, speaking into his mic as he turned away.

Not hanging around, Wren took her pack and blanket and box of Timbits, heading for an exit, vowing she was never getting married. No way she was ending up with a guy like her dad, or worse, like Kevin Snow. Till death do us part, vows made in a moment that couldn't last the rest of your life. Then there was the sex, and she was mildly curious, but wasn't totally convinced about it either. Seemed kind of messy. She'd seen the male equipment once, the kid next door, Brendan, having one of those "I'll show you mine, you show me yours" moments. Told him she wasn't playing, but out it came anyway. Not sure why he was proud of something that had the appeal of a banana slug. Told him so, and explained the look of it was the very reason adults turned the lights off when they did it. Brendan kept it in his pants after that. Maybe she'd ruined the kid for life.

Biting into a blueberry Timbit, she got out of there, leaving Sea Island, eating the tiny donuts one by one, saving the lemon for last. The cold of night stabbed like teeth through the hoodie, Wren crossing over the Fraser, the breeze harsh and stinging to the bone. Top it off, heavy clouds were rolling off the Pacific. The back street she walked was abandoned at this hour, Wren passing under a streetlight, going around back of an unlit lube-and-oil joint, trying to get out of the wet and wind, she set her stuff down, trying the back door handle just as a car drove into the lot, some guy coming to start his early shift, the headlights catching her by the door.

The guy leaned over the wheel, taking a closer look through the windshield. Rolled down his window halfway and asked, "I help you?" Taking his cell phone in hand, set to call it in.

"Can stop blinding me for a start," she said. Raising a hand to shield her eyes against the glare. If he tapped in those three numbers, she was grabbing her stuff and running.

What he did, he swung the Hyundai into the spot by the

door, shutting off the lights and engine. Getting out, still holding his phone. Acne-scarred face and geeky looking, in his early twenties. "Still asking what you want?"

"Well, the truth is, I was hoping to use your ladies'; I'm in a bit of a pickle." Pressing her knees together. Wren thinking it was the universal sign for "I need to pee."

"A what?"

"Lady business." Putting a hand on her hip, making like she was talking to a dumbbell. Another thing her mom had told her: thoughts of "lady business" usually scared the hell out of men.

"Oh, sure, uh, guess that's fine . . ." Slipping the phone into his pocket, he went to the door, getting his ring of keys, selecting the right one. Getting the door open, tapping in the alarm code on a panel, waiting on the red light to go green. Turning on the lights and telling her it was straight ahead, first door to the left.

Leaving her stuff by the door, she headed for the hallway, the guy busied himself, getting the place ready, switching on more lights. Willy in the morning coming on a portable radio, a fuzzy FM signal. Like all radio personalities, this Willy must have thought he was funny.

"That come with coffee?" she called, smiling over her shoulder, going down the hall.

"Lemme get the water on. Warn you though, it's just Yuban."

"Long as it's hot." Wren's smile widened, working the charm. "Appreciate it, uh . . ." Waiting on him to say his name — Jeff. Saying her name, sure as she turned left, he wasn't punching 9-1-1, the two of them on a first-name basis now. Trusting him with her stuff.

"This it, Jeff?" Pointing at a door.

"Yeah. Other one's just brooms and stuff. And sorry, never got to mopping it out last night. Could be a bit, you know — funky."

"You got to go, you got to . . ." Stopped as she stepped in, flicking the light switch, like a cockroach warning device. "Ohh!" Sucking her breath — crawlies with many legs diving in cracks and holes. Jeff wasn't kidding, not mopping it out being an understatement, the place foul and fusty, the waste bin spilling with paper towel, a toilet roll unfurled across the floor. The tap at the sink was dripping with the flu. Unsnapping the brass button, pulling the zip and pushing down her jeans, she hovered above the seat, not making contact with the porcelain. Praying nothing in the bowl could jump.

Didn't dry herself, lifting a sneaker to flush. Couldn't tug the denim up fast enough, stepping over the line of toilet tissue, careful not to slip. No way she was going down on this floor. All the crawlies likely to jump on her. Elbowing the light switch, and twisting the knob with her sleeve, she was out and going back down the hall.

"You been in there lately, Jeff? Things crawling in there say they're not voting you employee of the month."

"I tried to warn you." Jeff gave a weak smile.

"Place could make Mr. Clean hurl."

"Thing of it is, I got hired to change the oil. Can see I already got four waiting, right? And we're not open for a couple of hours yet." Pointing to a Civic up on the lift, three more cars lined out front of the double garage door. "Company's got a kid starting next week. Means I'm getting a bump-up, and not sure the kid knows it yet, but he's on toilets."

"He get danger pay?"

"It'll teach him to drop out, huh?" Jeff grinned.

"It's not so bad, the job, I mean."

"It's okay. I like to monkey with cars, always have. For now, it's just changing oil and filters, doing the lube. But I'm signing for some courses, become a service technician down the road. Pays pretty good."

"Next time I see you, I could be in for a better cup." Wren smiled, thinking this guy was alright and had some ambition.

"Guess so." Jeff brightened at the prospect of seeing her again. Saying, "You like it strong, the coffee?" Lining up a couple of mugs, checking to see if they were clean. "I think we got some styro cups."

"Yeah, take-out would be better." Thinking if she looked close, the mugs in this place might look like the toilet, cleaned by the same guy.

Going to the cupboard, he searched around, finding a plastic sleeve, saying, "I was hoping you'd stay."

"How about the four cars waiting?"

"Let them wait." Jeff's face flushed, making the acne light up.

Wren wondering about his age, eighteen, maybe nineteen.

The electric kettle sputtered behind him, Jeff tending to it, spooning coffee, offering powdered creamer and packets of sugar. Talked about going to community college. Wren sharing the last two Timbits, telling how she was new in town, talked some about where she was from, and not sure how long she was staying.

"You mind me asking, how old you are?"

"Old enough."

Jeff was refilling her styro with water, mixing in more instant. Hinting that he had a pull-out couch at his crib, just a quick bus ride, down the No. 5 Road. "I mean, just till you get on your feet."

Wren thinking of what could be living in the folds of his pull-out. Said she'd been making friends since she left back east, getting here yesterday, mentioning Maude, then Jade and Patch. All of them offering her a place to crash.

"Yeah, folks here are West Coast friendly. Well, mostly anyway."

"Well, it's nice of you, and I appreciate the offer." Wren seeing this guy's kindness, and the loneliness behind it. Nothing she was ready for. And remembering what her mom said about men having this thing, like a struggle between urge and conscience, conscience usually drawing second.

Taking a pen, Jeff wrote his number on the side of her take-out cup, the pen inscribing the styro. "So you know where to find me. I mean, in case . . ."

She put it in her backpack, told him she didn't have a number to give him, and asked how close she was to the casino.

"The Rock?" Jeff looked past the garage doors, pointing along the road, showing the way, less than half a mile. Not asking why she wanted to know.

Finishing her second cup, she swung the strap of the backpack over a shoulder, grabbed the blanket and got set to go.

"Guess you know where to find me," Jeff said, looked at the waiting cars.

"Yeah, maybe I'll call you." And she thanked him.

Walking the No. 3 Road, she turned where he told her, passing the casino with its fountain gurgling and statue washed in red and green floodlights. Shrugging into the hoodie from the damp, she went into the parking garage, seven floors of concrete and cars. Stepping between the rows, she checked door handles, searching for one left unlocked. Wren shaking, thinking she could've used a third cup of Jeff's coffee.

Didn't know anything about gambling, just it was something that grown-ups did when they drank booze. Wren picturing them with cards and dice and getting drunk. Her best guess, at this hour most of them would be crashed out. Likely be noon before the place showed any signs of life. Meaning she had time to sneak a nap.

« « «

And now there she was, trapped behind the backseat of the moving SUV, careful to keep her breathing quiet. Nothing West Coast friendly about the two men up front, and getting caught would mean something awful. No doubt in her mind. Not allowing thoughts of getting dragged away by the two men, doing horrible things to her. A fat needle plunged into her arm, and she'd be lost to them, and they'd control her, do what they wanted. That fear was worse than any thought of Kevin Snow putting his hands on her.

Behind the rear seat, she felt the vehicle sway. Hearing the two men talking up front, bragging about robbing somebody at the casino, laughing about it. The stolen cash in a couple of bags, the one called Angel holding on to them.

Fifteen years old and Wren had a feeling it could be over before it got started. Maybe Robin was right about being out here on her own. Back behind the seat, the interior filled with smoke. And she felt her stomach flip, and finally she coughed. Grabbed her backpack and pushed up the rear gate as the brakes squealed, and she jumped out and ran for her life. Leaving the blanket behind. Running flat out, looking behind her, catching her breath in a small park, taking a footbridge over a creek, going into the back of some other mall. Not sure if the two men got a good look at her, she walked into the public can, got in the far cubicle, set down the pack, thought a minute, tugged off her hoodie and hung it on the hook. Leaving the door latched, she crawled under the stall, then walked into Urban Planet, doing it like she had all day to shop, looking at some racks, telling the sales lady she was just browsing, looking to spend some birthday money an aunt had sent. Trying on a faux-fur bomber in mauve, then she checked a black ball cap in a mirror, seeing the reflection of the sales lady busy behind her at a rack of new arrivals. Then Wren walked out with her new outfit, ready to run, but nobody spotted her.

Back in the washroom, she reached under the stall for her pack, left the hoodie, reapplied the lipstick in the washroom mirror, tucked her hair under the cap, and left. If the creeps got a look at her, they wouldn't recognize her now. And she walked out, went back over the footbridge, walked up to Marine and started west. Wanting something hot to eat to help keep her warm. The McDonald's lineup was right to the door, and the food wasn't worth waiting in a line. Wren reached in a pocket and counted her cash.

A woman walked along leading a small dog, the Boston terrier tugging on its leash, a joy-bubble of fur, jumping up Wren's leg. The woman apologized for its behavior as Wren bent to it, asking its name, giggling and getting doggy-kissed, the stub of a tail wagging like mad. Covering the dog's ears as an ambulance passed, Wren asked the woman about a good place to eat, along with directions to downtown. The woman pointed down Lloyd, told her the Potlatch was the best place around. Told her which bus would take her to Lonsdale Quay, where the SeaBus crossed to downtown.

"That a one- or two-zone ride, you know?" Wren learning how the transit worked.

Reaching in her handbag, the woman said she wasn't sure about the fare, and it was none of her business to ask questions, so she wouldn't, holding out some cash.

"I'm fine, really." Wren guessed in spite of the new jacket and hat she looked worse than she thought, thanking the woman anyway.

The woman insisting, Wren shrugging, taking the bills and thanking her.

"And if there's somebody you'd like me to call ..."

"There's nobody. I'm good, really." Wren hesitated, pocketed the money, thanked the woman and patted the little dog, saying it was like sunshine. Worth any allergic reaction. Then she was crossing at the lights, not looking back. Not at all sure why she was crying again. Maybe she was losing her mind.

Pretty sure this was the same street where she jumped out of the SUV, guessing it happened over an hour ago. The two creeps long gone, likely off counting their stolen loot.

The restaurant was small and angled from the street with totems out front, painted in red, black and white. The aroma of the place drew her in, Wren thinking the twenty the woman gave her would cover a good meal, one that would keep her going all day. The specials board by the door told her the big deal today was meatloaf. Wren remembering how her mom made it, with the baked ketchup top. Feeling the past well up inside, telling herself not to cry. Pinching herself.

"Hard to say no to that." An old man shuffled up behind her, coming from the parking lot in back and scaring her out of her sneakers. His saggy cheeks pulled up into a smile, deep creases across his forehead. Putting his weight on a walking stick, he said he was sorry to startle her. If he noticed she'd been crying, he didn't show it. Holding the door for her, he said, "Go for the meatloaf, miss, a word to the wise." And gave a friendly wink.

Smiling back, she went in, relaxing in the warmth of the place. The aroma had her realizing how hungry she was. A couple was finishing lunch near the door, the man checking the tab. Two men sat at the counter, their backs to her, hunkered over their plates.

The waitress asked how many, and Wren said one, then something dumb about her mom meeting her here, thinking she might look too young to be alone. The waitress telling her to park anywhere she liked. Then turned to the old man who she knew as a regular, asking, "Let me guess, having the usual, Fitch?"

"You read my mind, Dell. But seeing that smile's reason enough. Oh, and let's double up on the garlic bread today." Rubbing his hands together, Fitch said hello to the couple on his way past Wren, said something to the cook through the pass window, shuffling to the corner spot, laying the walking stick across from him and easing himself onto the seat.

Wren sat at the table closest to the door, set the backpack on the floor next to her, accepted a menu and read it while the waitress took the payment from the other couple, brought the old man coffee along with the day's *Globe*, doing it without being asked. She came back and asked Wren if she needed a few more minutes.

Fitch put a hand to the side of his mouth, whispered to her, "Remember the meatloaf."

Dell saying, "Fitch here's what we call a broken record, stuck on the one track, won't try nothing new. And trust me, everything here's worth trying."

"Well, meatloaf does sound good," Wren said, asking what it came with, looking over, seeing the old man give an approving nod, then he flapped up the newspaper, and flipped through a section. Wren glanced to the clock on the far wall, noticed the two men hunkered over their plates at the counter, one glancing over. And she felt a chill. Nearly made her jump.

"Comes with garlic bread and veg of the day," Dell said. "Today it's steamed broccoli."

Wren nodded without hearing what the woman said. Had only seen the back of their heads from behind the rear seat. The one driving wearing a round hat, like the guy at the counter looking over. Meaning, he was Angel. She was sure of it, forcing herself not to run out the door, looking out the window, acting casual, then glancing at the washroom sign, hoping there was a back way out. Told the waitress she'd be right back in case her mom came in, leaving her backpack and walking past the men without a look. Both of them holding giant burgers, the one called Angel leaning so when his patty dripped, it dripped on his plate, not on his shirt. The one called Cooder had no such concern. Neither looked up as she passed on the way to the ladies' room.

... *the Potlatch*

L ifting an arm and giving a sniff, Cooder looked at Angel, saying, "Weird, huh?" Biting into his burger, his cheek puffed full, his jaw going up and down.

Angel ran a fry through a puddle of ketchup on his plate and ate it, aware of the kid going past them to the can. He'd been thinking of their score: a hundred grand in one bag, ten in the other, along with a few hundred in chips. At first, he figured the kid came in with the old man, then she told the waitress she was meeting her mom. Trying to remember the one jumping and running from the Expedition, sure she had on a black jacket, maybe a hoodie. Never got a good look, wasn't even sure if it was a girl, just remembered the long hair and dark clothes, nothing like this kid was wearing, this kid with her hair tucked under a ball cap. But still . . .

"One pit's like *pew*, off the charts, guess from the excitement . . ." Cooder doing his sniff test with the left arm up, saying, "Left one's fine."

"The fuck are you talking about?"

"Saying how one pit's stronger'n the other. Think it's weird."

"Yeah, good to know, especially when I'm eating," Angel dipped another fry in ketchup, looking around, just the old man in the corner hidden behind his paper, a blue-collar guy coming in and sitting at the end of the counter, likely on his lunch break, overalls with his name scripted on the breast pocket, the waitress going to him and handing him a menu. Angel leaning close to Cooder, saying, "You see the kid?"

"What kid?"

"Yeah, right."

"How're the burgers, fellas?" Dell swung by with a smile — happier customers meant bigger tips. "Top you up if you want?" Meaning the coffee.

Cooder nodded, talking around his puffed cheek, saying, "These burgers, man, just like the Chief said." Using his tongue to maneuver food around, his lips wet with grease. Coming up for air between bites.

"Good to hear." Dell saying, "Dessert measures up too, in case you fellas left room. Today it's cream pie or chocolate pudding, both made in-house."

Cooder shook his head and said, "Only place I could put it's in my pocket."

Dell gave him a look that said she didn't doubt he'd do it, then looked to Angel.

"Maybe another time," Angel said, still wondering about the kid. Waiting till the waitress moved off, the cook in back hitting a bell, beckoning Dell to the pass window. The old boy's meatloaf was up.

"Think it's our kid." Angel kept his voice down, thinking she could be calling the cops.

Cooder shook his head, sure it wasn't the kid, the look all wrong. Working his jaws, elbows planted on either side of his plate, intent on finishing, saying, "Lemme enjoy this."

"Leave a tip," Angel said and got up, acting nonchalant, looking to Dell. "Washroom?" His thumb going to the sign with the arrow.

Dell nodded, getting the plate from the pass window, along with a small basket of garlic bread.

Cooder kept chewing, saying to her, "Egg on top's a nice touch." A trace of yolk escaped down his stubbled chin.

Dell said it was good to hear.

Angel headed for the can, glancing over his shoulder. The old boy in the corner folding up the newspaper, the waitress sliding the plate in front of him, the other guy reading a menu, trying to decide.

« « «

"Here you go, Fitch. Cut you a nice thick one," Dell said to the old guy.

"You're the best, Dell."

"I know it."

Cooder's cell went off. Checking the display, he breathed, "Fuck me," and answered, sounding pleasant, "What's up, Muff?"

"We need to talk."

"Thought we did, middle of the Taco Bell."

"Except you didn't hear a word I said."

He rolled his eyes. The woman couldn't say sorry, slapping him in a public place — now giving him more attitude. Had a good idea what life with her would be like. Toss a screaming kid in the mix. No thank you.

"Think we need to see somebody," Tracy said from the phone.

"Like somebody else?" Cooder looked around, the waitress

talking to the old guy in the corner, the other guy drinking coffee. Angel in the can. The short-order cook stuck his head through the pass-through, calling for the waitress to fetch a can of PAM, needed it before she took her smoke break.

"What'd you say?" Tracy barked.

"I'm going along, how we ought to see somebody else."

"That's not what I . . . oh, you prick!"

The waitress walked by him, going to the supply room by the washrooms, getting knocked aside as Angel charged out of the ladies', calling to Cooder, "Let's go." Then hurrying out the door.

The whole world was mad. Cooder twisted his neck, watched Angel rush out, hearing Tracy yell through the phone. He didn't get what set her off — it was her fucking idea.

Switching off his phone, he resisted tossing it to the floor and stomping on it, telling the waitress, "The Chief was right." Giving her a thumbs up, then going out the door.

The waitress calling after him about the unpaid tab.

« « «

Taking that first bite, Fitch watched the shorter man dash from the can, nearly knocked Dell over, called to his buddy and was out of there. The same two guys he saw down at the dog park, had recognized them when he came in, still trying to put their story together, an old habit from his cop days. The bigger guy followed his buddy out, forgetting to pay, Fitch taking another bite.

Dell came from the supply room, a can of cooking spray in hand, looking bewildered. Taking the plate of garlic bread, she set it in front of Fitch.

"What's wrong?" he said.

"That girl climbed out the window." Dell confused, seeing her backpack by her chair, saying, "Usually you eat first, then duck the check. Like them two."

Reaching his walking stick, Fitch pushed himself up, saying, "Be a dear and stick this under the lamp." Taking the can of cooking spray from her, he asked for her lighter, and he was hobbling for the door, saying, "Be right back."

Hardly touched his meatloaf, left Dell holding the plate, wondering what the hell was going on, everybody running out without paying, but he had no time to explain.

. . . *the boondocker*

Out back of the place, Angel caught the kid dangling from the ledge, dropping from the window. Grabbing hold of her arm, he jerked her around. "Gotcha."

"Hey, you're hurting me!" she was yelling, struggling to break the hold. His hand clapping over her mouth. She squirmed, tried to bite, then kicked his shin.

"Little bitch." Angel swung her against the concrete wall, knocking the air from her.

Coming around the side, Cooder saw what was going on, eyed the lot, just the Expedition and an old RV. "Jesus H. . . . ." Sure it was the wrong kid.

Angel yelling at him, "Hurry the fuck up!"

Using the device, Cooder popped the locks, getting behind the wheel. Reaching over the seat, belching and pushing open the back door.

Biting the hand, the girl tried to yell, getting smacked by Angel, fighting to keep from getting shoved inside.

Knocking away the cap, Angel clutched her hair, threw her against the Ford, the girl all arms and legs and full of fight. Kicking at the door, she twisted and growled.

Hitting and grabbing, Angel twisted her and shoved her at the door. If he hadn't ditched the pistol at his place, he would have pulled it.

Starting the engine, Cooder was getting the hell out of there. Tearing off his jacket, he flung it over the seat, saying, "Bag her up." Goddamn psycho partner abducting the wrong kid.

Grabbing the jacket, Angel got it over her head. Taking another kick to his shin.

« « «

Panicked. Too winded to scream now. She felt herself pushed across the seat, tried to get her heel up to buck at him — no way — swatting at the jacket thrown over her head. Fighting with everything she had, feeling herself losing, but not stopping. Clawing at the hands, trying again to bite. Felt herself grabbed by the hair, from behind, the one called Cooder leaning over the seat, twisting her around, her eyes watering from the pain. Grabbed at the jacket he tried to put over her. Shooting out a sneaker, hearing the other one yelp in pain. Her fingers digging into the top of Cooder's hands, feeling his skin under her fingernails. The big man punched at her head through the jacket, lost his hold for a moment. Catching a flicker of daylight, she was seeing the old man coming behind Angel. Thinking he was coming with the needle. Saw he had a can in one hand, raising a stick in the other.

« « «

Fitch struck the man with his crutch, a thump across the spine, then tossed it down and took a step back.

"What the fuck —" The dark-haired one cringed and turned on him.

Fitch had the spray can raised, the guy letting go of the girl, coming at him, set to tear him apart. The one behind the wheel leaned halfway over the seat, pinning the kid down.

Fitch had the lighter and flicked it.

"You dead fuck —" The guy grabbing for him.

The spray whooshing like a fireball, the guy snapping his head back and letting go of Fitch, both hands clutching for his own face, screaming as he twisted and went to his knees.

Swatting away the jacket, the girl broke free and jumped out past the man going to his knees.

Bending for his walking stick, Fitch told her, "Get in." Pointing to the RV.

The big man lost the hat climbing over the console, squeezing between the seats, shoving his buddy out of the way, saying, "I got this."

Hurrying behind her, then hoicking the door handle, Fitch pushed the girl inside, getting in, locking the door behind him, pushing her out of his way, getting behind the wheel.

The dark-haired one was bawling by the Expedition, his eyes like stoplights. He was up and stumbling blind, trying to blink away the pain.

Fitch cranked the key, the big man catching up and whomping his fist against the RV's door, smashing the passenger glass, reaching in and grabbing for the handle.

Slapping it in reverse, Fitch yelled to the girl, "Get down." Mashing the gas pedal, he heard the yelp, the big man being arm-dragged and knocked clear.

Blinking like mad, the other guy saw Fitch's spare tire cover, Happy Camper, rushing at him. Jumping out of the way as the RV T-boned the big Ford, bucking it against the cinder blocks, caving its side like a beer can.

Fitch was slammed into the seat back, the girl tossed down and sliding to the rear along the RVs floor. Shifting, Fitch pulled forward, the sound of scraping metal as the vehicles parted. The Winnebago on wobbling wheels, Fitch thinking his ride took the worst of it.

Scrambling up, the big man grabbed a handful of gravel and flung it after the RV. Fitch hearing it clatter against the tail end, driving out of there.

« « «

Happy Camper is what he saw, the old man peeling away. Cooder couldn't believe it, his elbows and knees stinging and scraped, his pants torn. Looking around at Angel.

"Fuck!" Angel blinking his red eyes. "Fuck me." Getting the passenger door open and pulling himself onto the seat. "Fuck!"

The Expedition was crying fluids, pressed against the cinder blocks. Practically had to drag his leg, Cooder went to the crunched back door, unable to shut it.

Pulling Angel back out, he got in the passenger door and started to climb over the console.

Dell the waitress came around the side, followed by the cook. "What the hell?"

"Blind old fuck can't drive worth shit. Look at this." Cooder said, getting back out and pointing to the damaged side.

Angel rubbing his red eyes.

The waitress held up their tab, waiting on explanation.

Both of them looking at her, then at each other, both patting their pockets, neither bringing enough of the casino money to cover lunch.

The cook turned for the totems, said he was calling the

cops. Dell saw the can of PAM on the ground, retrieved it along with her lighter and went in after him.

"Get the fuck in." Squeezing between the seats, Cooder scrambled over the console, got behind the wheel, using the transmitter to start the ignition, looking at Angel, saying, "Good work, you got her, fucktard." Cooder grinned, thinking he had plenty to say anytime Angel brought up the scene at the casino, about Cooder getting knocked down, and Angel jumping in and saving the day.

No way to close the smashed door, he scraped the Expedition off the cinder blocks, the sound of grinding metal, leaving a streak of black paint on the blocks, and hauling out of there. No way they were getting any cash for this ride. He'd have to wipe it down and dump it.

"Fuck me." Angel cupped his eyes, said he needed Visine.

"Hurts, huh?" Cooder smiled at the rearview, thinking the loss on the Ford was coming out of Angel's end. Felt like it was limping from the alley, Cooder pulled down Pemberton and hung a left at the first street, looking at his torn and bloody sleeve, saying, "One thing's sure, that happy camper's got serious payback coming."

Angel moaning.

« « «

"You alright?" Nosing the RV into traffic and rolling east on Marine, passing the mall, the old Sears store, the wall smudged where the lettering had been. Turning to the girl, looking concerned, Fitch asked her again.

"Mister, don't even look at me funny . . ." Brushing glass from the passenger seat, facing him, the girl full of fight.

"Can't help looking funny." He took a breath, his pulse racing, a knot like a throb in his neck. "Take a minute, miss, and tell the good guys from the bad, okay? I know it went pretty fast. I'm trying to catch up myself."

"No cops." She looked like she was set to jump.

"You saw what I did, right? Dangerous driving, criminal negligence, child endangerment . . ."

"I'm not a child."

"Okay, how about assault with a flame thrower?"

She just looked at him.

"Any idea of the demerit points alone? Not to mention, seniors have to report for license review every twelve months, prove we're not a menace."

"So no cops?"

"No cops." Fitch drew more air, trying to ease his pounding heart, keeping the rig in the lane — not the time to tell her he'd put twenty years on the job, the retired shield in his wallet.

In spite of the cold rushing through the busted window, the girl settled on the seat, saying, "You in a circus or something? That thing you did."

"With the spray?"

"Yeah."

"Improvising."

"Well . . ."

"Pretty cool, right?"

"I guess so." She relaxed some, saying, "The stuff of superheroes."

Maybe she didn't see a grandpa with liver spots and sagging flesh. Cap'n Colostomy. Fitch smiled and said, "Tell the truth, I wasn't thinking too much of anything." Nodding to his walking stick laying between the seats. Adding, "Nothing like a nice piece of hickory." When she didn't react, he told her it was a line from a movie. "You know, Clint Eastwood?"

"Uh uhn."

"Well, thought maybe you . . . just a guy in the movies."

"Think he's like you?" She reached his stick and leaned it behind his seat, looked like she was starting to ease. Saying, "Kind of remind me of that guy, you know, the one from *Grumpy Old Men*. The funny-looking one." Touching her head, a little blood coming from her scalp.

"That's Matthau. And thanks, I guess. Sure you're not . . . forget it." Smiling, saying, "Anyway, nice to meet you, miss . . ."

"Call me Penny."

"And I'm Fitch. Nice to meet you, Penny."

"And thanks for that, the lift. Any place you can pull over's fine." She lifted a sneaker, retying her lace.

"The lift?"

"Yeah, thanks. Here's fine."

"Not as fine as you think. Dollars to donuts, they're coming after us." Fitch not sure he immobilized them. "You want out, not a problem, but let me get you where it's safe. And maybe let me take a look at that cut."

Putting a hand to her head, she looked at the streak of red on her finger. She put the hand on the door handle, said she'd be fine, then turned to the rear of the RV like somebody might be hiding back there. Then she was looking at the bag showing from under his shirt, like she was wondering what the hell it was. Fitch saying, "A colostomy bag, and I'm not afraid to use it."

She smiled, was clearly afraid to ask, and looked out at the road, the direction he was taking her. Saying, "Here's fine, really."

"Look, Penny, I know you're scared. Guess I am too. And you've likely got more questions than answers right now, but so you know, I'm not your worry. You want out, that's no problem, but how about you wait till it's safe. Okay?" He glanced at his side-view mirror, felt a shaking from the back end, could be the alignment, or the frame got twisted. "Let me ask you something: you got any idea who those guys are?"

"Nope."

"You got somebody I can call, like a parent?"

"That's a need-to-know basis."

"Uh huh. The strong independent type, okay, I get it. And that's good you can take care of yourself." No point in asking questions. Turning down Fell, he drove past the Auto Mall, a dozen car dealers and a sea of chrome and sheet metal. At Harbourside, he turned right and looped around the vacant parcel of land. The private school to the west, the Burrard Yacht Club to the east, the inlet with its freighters and anchored barges, the city across the inlet.

Four faded RVs sat parked along the streets ringing the dry grass and weeds. Fitch pulled past a camper, along a line of boulevard trees, and backed into a spot. The camper behind them had Open Road on its front grill, most of its body stripe faded to a dull pink, pale curtains drawn across the windshield, a roof vent and its side window open.

Wren had her hand on the door handle, eager to get out.

Not making a move to stop her, Fitch said, "Good a spot as any."

"What is this place?" Hesitating, she looked to the harbor, a freighter out past a paddle wheeler taking tourists around a couple of anchored barges. A couple walking a beagle, masts rising above the Burrard Yacht Club.

"A better one than you were in." Keying off the engine, he said the worst part was leaving his meatloaf half-finished. Asked what she had ordered, nodded when she said she ordered the same, on his recommendation. Thinking of the saucy crust glazed on top, criminis, peppers, onions, minced sirloin, broccoli on the side. Enough to make an old man weep.

Doing it slow, he leaned close and had a look at her cut; not too bad, no need for stitches. Pushing himself out of the seat and going to the tiny kitchen area, grateful his hip held up, although it was aching from the action-hero moves back in the Potlatch's lot. He got the first-aid travel pack, the little bottle of iodine, and held them out. The girl taking them from him, saying she could do it. Fitch pointed to the sink and the side-view mirror. Noticing the sales tag hanging from her faux-fur jacket.

"Bet it was pretty good, huh, the meatloaf?" she said, going to the door, leaning out the broken window, using the big side mirror, not bothering with the iodine, just sticking a small bandage over the cut.

Fitch guessing she was still deciding whether she could trust him. "You want to run, I'm too old to stop you."

"Didn't look too old back there." She handed back the first-aid stuff.

"That was dumb luck. And those two were even dumber. Just one thing, you're welcome to hang around, but let's do it on a first-name basis, okay?"

"Already told you it's Penny."

"No, it's not."

"How come?"

"You got a *W* on the bottom of your shoes." He'd seen it when she tied her sneaker, the kind of thing his daughter, Carolyn, did back when she was in grade school, writing her initials on them, kept the other kids from boosting her gym shoes. He went to a cupboard, taking down a can of stew, about to offer her lunch. "More like a Wendy, Wanda, Winifred, Wilhelmina. Let me know when I'm getting warm."

She tipped her foot and looked at the bottom of her shoe. And like that, she threw open the door and sprang out and was gone.

Fitch frowned, thinking he asked too many questions — putting the family-size Dinty Moore back, and taking out a single-serve of Campbell's.

. . . *liver spots and runaways*

That old guy, Fitch, was sharp for a grandpa, walked with a stick, and what was with that gross bag? Took care of the creeps and monster-trucked their ride. Drove out of there, acting like nothing had happened. Wren hoped his ticker held up, wondered how old he was, over fifty, maybe older — the guy had liver spots. Hoping his camper was alright too. It was dented in the back, and she thought it made scraping sounds when they drove away. Not sure why she ran from him.

Remembering the directions the woman with the little dog gave her earlier, Wren passed a marina, a line of floating homes, a park with kids climbing on an iron sculpture, treating it like a play apparatus. Making her way to Lonsdale Quay, a busy hub with teens hanging around a Mickey D's, passengers lined at a kiosk, topping up their transit cards. A two-bit jeweler, a pizza joint, some kids' store with a bubble blower outside, a brewpub with a busy courtyard. Going past the eateries inside, thinking of the meatloaf she missed out on, she bought a gyro, found a bench, sat and ate, looking out at the dancing water. The SeaBus crossed the inlet, filled with silhouettes of passengers. Could get on the next one and sail to the downtown side, look up Jade and Patch. Wondering if Maude was at the Fairmont's spa with a mask on her face and cucumber slices over her eyes.

Just needed a next move, but what happened behind the restaurant had her rattled and looking over her shoulder. She was more kid than adult now, and she was alone, getting flashes of her mom toward the end, that look of giving up. And then she was gone. Thoughts of the mother-and-daughter things they'd never do. One day there, all the time in the world, the two of them talking over bowls of Ben & Jerry's, watching *Fried Green Tomatoes* for about the twentieth time — safe in that world.

No tears this time. She was angry, and she hated drugs, and she hated her dud dad for turning the world upside down, not thinking of him as Dad anymore. Wanted to call him up and say how she felt, tell him she was never coming to live with him — like ever.

Watching the SeaBus dock, Wren decided what to do, getting up and walking out of there.

« « «

Switching on the radio inside the RV, the weather report promising showers, then some pop diva called Lady some-thing caterwauling to a synthesized drum beat. What passed as music. Whatever happened to Peggy Lee? And Ella and Patsy? Women with class, singing about wanting to be wanted, and making you believe it. Fitch switched it off. The hell happened to the rainbow? Best station, playing the best music back before somebody branded it oldies. Nowadays heavy metal played across the oldie airwaves. Where did that push the good stuff? Dean and Frank and Tony. Carmen McRae and Walter Wanderley and his smooth samba.

Spooning up his supper cereal, he was back to thinking of making the run to Peachland. Yeah, with any luck he'd freeze his ass through one more Peachland winter, something he swore he'd never do again, but this was the last chance to see Carolyn. And if any kind of luck held, he'd be around for the new baby, get to hold his grandchild in his arms. Remembered holding Carolyn the day she was born. The pink fingers and toes and that sweet baby smell.

Before rolling, his home on wheels needed some TLC, the Winnebago Brave had taken a beating, its back end mashed up, the bumper cracked and twisted, the chrome ladder crushed, the taillight gone. Could be some damage underneath too.

He'd get Marty at Norseman's garage to have a look and do enough to get him on the road. The good news was, the old engine had a solid heartbeat, the rebuilt tranny had given him no worries, and the Dunlops had enough tread for the job as long as he got ahead of the coming winter.

Like that, he was done with boondocking and living on the road. The visit to Russell's office made definite what he already knew anyway. Meaning there would be no waiting list for some assisted-living place, something that had sat heavy on his mind, not wanting to end up in a place like that. With time slipping away, he'd go back to the house he'd left to Carolyn, the five acres in Peachland, and he'd live out his days and try not to be a nuisance.

Felt good leaving her the place, and he was sure it would be worth something the day they pushed that proposed highway bypass through. And she'd get whatever else he had squirreled in the savings, along with the Brave.

He dried and put away the dishes, duct-taped cardboard over the busted window, and drew the curtains across the windshield. He sat on the pull-down, switched on the lamp and read a few pages from the *Reader's Digest* — a dog-eared copy somebody left when they moved on — a story set in California around the time of the quake of '06, a young man starting out with nothing and setting out to make his fortune, falling for the daughter of a land baron. Backwards and back-woods, the hero was getting to understanding about the rich girl's game. Fitch thinking back how it took him a couple tries before he got women halfway right, how to be with them. Then along came Annie, and made the understanding easy as a sea breeze. And any rough spots, well, she smoothed them out, and life had been good. Yeah, he'd been a lucky man. Not sure how he would have ended up without her. He got the better end of the deal, that's for sure. Married to Annie Ruth Haut for forty-three years, till that cabbie fell asleep at the wheel, losing control. Now it was his turn. Goddamn cancer — something he could really swing his stick at.

Setting the *Reader's Digest* on his stomach, his eyes too tired for reading, Fitch wondering about the kid, name starting with *W* — out there on her own. Running from something besides those two clowns, likely from some home-life hell. Something he had dreaded bumping up against when he was on the force. Nothing worse than stepping into a situation of child abuse, right up there with domestic dispute.

Feeling himself drift, he set his readers in the case, got his toothbrush and cup and squeezed on the Colgate. Spitting in the sink, seeing some blood in the foam. Looked at Methuselah in the mirror, telling himself to go to bed. It had been one hell of a day, going to the oncologist, missing out on meatloaf, and taking care of the assholes — getting into his pajamas when he heard the scrape of shoes on the pavement outside. First thought, they found him. Reaching the .22 from under the pull-down, the one he took from a Park Gang thug all those years ago, the guy long gone and the piece long forgotten, its serials filed down — not the heft of the duty weapon he once carried, but enough caliber to get the job done. Slipping on the housecoat, he dropped the pistol in the pocket, went and put a finger to the side curtain and checked outside, tiptoeing to the front, tying the sash over the colostomy bag, saying through the busted window, now taped over in cardboard, "Better not be the Jehovahs."

« « «

"Sorry I ran off." She looked up at him, giving him sheepish.

"You don't owe me a reason." The small-cal in his house-coat pocket, he pushed open the door, inviting her back in. Wished he'd shoved his feet into the SoftMocs. Hated the way his toes looked, that fungus, the big toenail ingrown and yellow, all the creams he bought doing squat.

She stepped past him, caught the way he was looking out, then closing the broken door behind her.

"I woke you, didn't I?"

"Figure us old people hit the hay before dark?"

"No, nothing like that."

Taking the walking stick from behind the driver's seat where she'd leaned it, he smiled and said he'd been busy dancing to his James Bond soundtrack.

Making her smile too, telling him, "I had some things to work out."

Putting weight on the stick, he said, "You work up an appetite, all that thinking?"

"Well, I guess I could eat. I mean, if you're offering." She shrugged.

"Have a seat."

She looked around the Brave's twenty-one-foot interior. A place to sit wasn't jumping out at her.

He pointed to the pull-down seat, forgot he'd put it back up, and showed her how it worked. Then she watched him go to what he figured she thought of as the tiniest kitchen in the world.

"Think I should explain a few things," she said. "I got in their car at this casino — just a car with the door open. Got in to get warm, not to steal anything."

"Sure." Fitch holding back about a hundred questions.

"And I guess I got sleepy."

More questions piled up, but he nodded, let her take her time.

"Woke when I heard them coming, you see, and I couldn't get out, hid behind the seat and stayed low. They drove off with me in the back, hearing everything they said."

"Talking about what?"

"Think they robbed somebody. The one not driving smoked the whole way, saying he wanted to count the money, what they had in the bags. The other one said to wait. He smoked too, but not so much. The two of them laughing about beating up this man."

Fitch looked thoughtful, not asking what an underaged kid was doing at a casino, or why she'd been out all night. Not the time for playing the ex-cop with questions. Fitch likely to get her running out the door again.

"I didn't want to hear it, you know, be an accessory or something."

"Sure, I get that."

"So I stayed down. Guess I finally coughed. I couldn't help it. And they looked, and I jumped out and ran. No idea where I was then or where to go. Just kept going so they couldn't get me, finally hiding in some trees. Walked around this mall and ended up in the meatloaf place. Just never want to see them again."

"Me neither."

Wren watched him pick up the kettle from the floor, one of the things that got knocked around. Setting it on one of the two burners, he punched a fallen cushion and offered it. "How about that something to eat?" Rubbing his hands together, thinking what to offer her.

"You didn't call the cops?"

"Thought we covered that."

"Well, things change."

"No, I didn't call." Crossed a finger over his heart and smiled. "Just glad we're both here talking about it. How's the head?" Looking at her Band-Aid, Fitch saw some bruising.

"I'm good."

"Sure went flying when I nailed their ride."

"I got bounce."

"I can see that."

Finding the dust pan in the only cupboard, Fitch swept pieces of a broken mug he'd missed from under the table, stepping on the lever of a trash bin, the lid popping up. Dumping the pan, he put everything back, offering her a bowl of Fiber One, with the other half of his banana sliced on top. Saying, "Not as tasty as meatloaf, but it's easy going down, and keeps you regular."

She crinkled her nose.

He unlatched the pull-down table and went to the mini-fridge. His cell toned, and he clicked it on, saying, "Hey ya, Milt. Yeah, some kid selling cookies, Guides or something." Fitch winked at her. "Yeah, I'm all good. And thanks for keeping an eye. Sure, you bet. Appreciate it, pal. Yeah, you too." He rang off, setting the phone in its charger.

"You got a Block Watch thing?"

"Better than that, we got Milt." Rethinking the Fiber One, he bent to the Danby and pulled the door, making a mental note to get homo next time — no need to fret about cholesterol, no more 2 percent. Leaning in the freezer compartment, he pulled a couple of Stouffer's entrees. "Tonight we got chicken fried rice, or broccoli and cheddar bake? You ask me, it's a split decision."

Tightening her lips, thinking about it, she stabbed a finger at the cheddar bake.

"Wise choice." Reaching his specs, he checked the nuke time. Taking off the outer wrap and sliding the tray in the microwave, he set the timer and pressed start. Then he leaned back against the counter, looking at her and waiting.

Folding her thin arms, she said she'd eat, but then she better get going.

"You can look out for yourself, I get that. And it's not your fault you climbed in the wrong ride. But think about it, I'm the guy who saved your tukhus, remember? You got no worries with me."

Narrowing her eyes, she said, "Tukhus?"

Fitch grinned, saying, "Tukhus: nowadays you use it for twerking." Giving a slight pelvic move, hoping the colostomy bag didn't flop from under the shirt, scare the hell out of her.

And he had her laughing again, likely couldn't believe an old man rocking his hips like that.

"And you think I should stay?"

"Sure, I do."

"But where?"

He pointed to the bench under her. "Table folds up, pull that out, next thing you got the guest suite."

Wren looked at the seat, saying, "I don't want to be any trouble, really."

"I don't think you can help it." He smiled and the microwave beeped. He took out the tray, put it on an oven mitt, set it in front of her, and told her not to touch the edges, and to enjoy.

"You won't be doing your . . . tukhus-twerking?"

"I promise."

"Guess you're one of the good guys." She picked up the fork and dug in.

"Damn right."

She aimed the tines at him. "You swore."

"You mean 'damn'?"

"Uh huh." She explained how she grew up with a swear jar in the house, something her mom insisted on. Anybody in her home ever swore, they paid a dime. Kept a civil tongue in everybody's head. "It's how I grew up. Except nowadays it's a quarter."

"Jeez, a quarter, I'd go broke."

And she pointed the fork again.

"What? 'Jeez'?"

"Uh huh. It's using the Lord's name in vain. Costs a quarter."

"I'm on a pension."

"Better not swear, then."

"You're a hard kid." He watched her eat, wondered if he ever knew anybody on the force who didn't swear, then said, "Fresh out of cocoa, but how about a tea? Got black, and maybe a few packets of herbal."

"How about coffee, I mean if it's not . . ."

"What, trouble?" He rolled his eyes, putting on his Matthau.

"Uh huh." She grinned.

"No, no trouble." He liked this kid. Lifted the Nespresso from the lower cupboard, explained what it was, filled its tank from the water jug.

The kid apologizing, not meaning for him to go to any bother.

"Think of it as a chance to show off. And all I got to do is add water and it's done." Offering her a choice of Stormio or Melozio.

"You decide."

And he hit the preheat button, got a cup and slid it under the outlet, making a show of it, how easy it was — putting her at ease — popping the top of a capsule and set it in. Locked it and hit start. Stopped himself from twerking.

A couple of minutes and the RV filled with that nice aroma.

Setting a cup in front of her, he put her fork in the sink, tossed the tray and packaging in the trash. Fitch ejected the capsule, threw caution to the wind and fixed himself a cup. Got the 2 percent, found some sugar packets, along with a spoon, laid everything in front of her.

"This place is kinda cool." She looked around, a little more settled, liking the compact efficiency, telling him she just took it black. Asked if he always parked in this same spot.

"Be here till ten in the a.m., then home's got to move at least a hundred feet, get a new view every four hours."

"On account of parking tickets?"

"It's a game we play with bylaws, move before they come with their chalk and ticket books. That or get fined."

"And you don't mind being alone?"

"Who's alone? I've got friends all around, and the kind you can count on."

"Like the one on the phone?"

"Milt, yeah. He's one of the good guys. We look out for each other."

"So, this all your stuff?" Wren looked around as she tried her coffee, saying it was real good.

"Matter of fact I'm thinking of downsizing, getting rid of a few things." Nothing he was taking with him where he was going. "And that bump we took today saved me some of the trouble."

"Whatever broke, I'd be happy to replace it, at least chip in."

"Most valuable thing's right here and working just fine." Fitch patted the coffee machine, saying, "The life's not for everyone, but it suits me fine." With his savings and pensions, he could afford more, but he wanted to leave all that for Carolyn, and he hadn't been wanting for much in a long time.

"As long as you're happy."

"Yeah, I'm happy," he said. "How about you? See you travel pretty light too."

"Except I left my backpack at the restaurant."

"Yeah, I remember. Well, maybe we'll see what we can do about that."

"Mean we'll go get it?"

"That is if you're staying this time?"

"Guess I can. Place has everything, just needs a swear jar," she said.

"Not sure I can afford it with you around."

"Profanity shows a lack of character. My mom said that."

Taking another sip, he said, "My castle, my rules. You know that one." Smiling to show he was kidding.

"It'll do you good, I promise."

"Okay, just so we're clear, define 'swearing,' because I'm not so sure about 'damn.' I mean there's the obvious ones, you know the ones, but how about 'holy cow' or 'William Shatner?'"

"It's inferred." Although she looked doubtful on Shatner.

"How about 'poo on a stick'?"

"Oh, definitely, but who says that?" She couldn't help but laugh.

"Okay, how about 'shut the front door'?"

She shook her head, trying to keep a straight face. "You're just trying to sneak a few in."

"You write a thesis on this, something like that?"

"Just learned it from my mom."

"Well, I guess I better toss a rope on it then, and mend some bad habits." On top of everything that happened today, he was having coffee at this hour. Wouldn't be much sleep tonight, but that was okay, as long as Annie came by later.

Wren sipped, saying, "You ever go anywhere in this, your home on wheels?"

"Matter of fact, I drove to an appointment today, then went to lunch. Where I bumped into you, then bumped into your friends."

"Aside from bumping, I mean you ever go on a road trip, someplace, I don't know, interesting?"

"Went to Barstow last year."

"Where's that?"

"California."

"No kidding?" She practically shot up. "In this?"

"Once upon a time, I spent almost every winter driving the coast. Cannon Beach, wine country, Monterey Peninsula. And yes, in this." He gave a condensed version of driving places with Annie and Carolyn. Stopping for snapshots of Haystack Rock, riding dune buggies, watching the sunset at Arcadia Beach. Talked about going over the Rockies.

"'Boondocking,' you make that up?"

He pointed past the closed curtains over the windshield. "All the campers and RVs you see. It's what they call us, boondockers. What else would you call it?"

"Free parking."

"Well, call it what you will."

"Whatever it is, I'm real glad you showed at the restaurant."

"I was lured by the meatloaf."

"I never got to try it."

"Left mine too, a da— a real shame."

"Well, I owe you," she said. "So next time it's on me."

"I might take you up on that," Fitch said. "But maybe we best let some time pass before we both go back."

"And so you know, I can take care of myself. I mean, usually. Something I've been doing a long time."

"I've no doubt about it," Fitch said. "Matter of fact, my first impression when I saw you, I thought, now there's a kid that needs no adult supervision."

"Yeah, you know when I first saw you?" She waited for him to bite, saying, "I wondered why you were out with no caregiver. Next thing, you beat up those two guys."

"Really thought that?"

"Just kidding."

"Okay, next time it's on you, but so you know, I go for extra garlic bread with lots of butter." Then asking again how her coffee was.

"Already said, it's real good." Taking another swallow, then saying, "How did you know to come out after them?"

"Didn't need to tell me they were all wrong."

"Think they'll come back?"

He shook his head and lied, "They learned a lesson, but I'm calling my buddy Milt, ask him to keep an eye on the place."

"Is he . . ."

"What, old?"

"Was going to say a boondocker."

"Milt's like our Block Watch. The man never sleeps and always first to spot bylaws coming."

"I was just kidding about being old."

Fitch waved her off. "I don't bruise easy."

"More'n I can say for those two. Bet they didn't know what hit them."

"Damn right. Oh, sorry."

She frowned, said he really needed a swear jar, teach himself not to do it.

"You think it'd work, huh? I'm pretty set in my ways."

"Guaranteed."

"How much would I owe?"

"A quarter each time, let's see . . . so far, a buck."

"Jeez."

"Another quarter."

"Come on. The man's in the bible. You want, I can show you."

"You took his name in vain. It counts." She finished her coffee and said, "Don't worry, you'll get the hang of it." Then she said, "And how come you took the cover off the back? Said Happy Camper on it."

"You're one sharp cookie."

"It got wrecked, didn't it?"

"Usually take it off this time of year."

"Or in case they come, like they could know it."

"See what I mean, sharp. My money's on those two being dumb as stumps, but why take chances." Fitch turned so she wouldn't spot the pistol in the housecoat pocket.

"So, Happy Camper, that like your handle?"

"Tire cover came like that. Canadian Tire special. Me, I don't go for handles, never felt the need."

"Why do they do that, name their campers?"

"It's a to-each-his-own thing."

"What are some of them?"

"Well, there's the Youngs in their Club Collapso, the camper with the pop-top. Then we've got Milt in his Country Coach. Totally Hitched, and Wander Woman. A new couple just in from someplace called Eyebrow in the prairies, their rig called Wanderlust. Had a friend come through from Barstow a couple of months back, on his way to Red Deer, calls his rig Stupid Piece of . . . fudged the last word with asterisks."

"He drives around like that, a swear word on the back?"

"Seemed to me the man was proud about it." Fitch guessing this kid was pouring on the innocent a little thick, but he let her do it.

Looking around the tiny space again, she said, "Look, I really don't want to be any trouble."

Fitch smiled and nodded to the seat she was on, told her again it doubled as a bed. "Just got to pull it out. A little narrow, but it's comfy enough. And it's all yours, unless you get a better offer." He wagged his hand around. "And maybe, just maybe, I like the company."

"Now you're playing me."

"And you'll be safe."

"With Milt keeping an eye."

"Right." Fitch thinking he should call his buddy, ask him to watch, but then he'd have to explain everything, feeling too tired for it. Saying to her, "And now, this old boy's had a blinking long day, so if you don't mind . . ." He drained his cup, took her empty cup and set both in the sink.

"I could call you on that, 'blinking.'"

"No way." Grinning, Fitch said he better get to sleep while he was still solvent. Adding, "And swear jars used to be a nickel."

"Maybe when you were a kid. These days, a nickel would have no meaning."

"Well, I'm too bushed to argue." Smiling as he moved to the back, his hip aching more, his ankles swollen. Taking the Hudson's Bay blanket with the four stripes from the overhead bin, he got her settled on the pull-out, pointed toward the back, saying, "That's me, behind the curtain, what the coach builder calls the deluxe suite." Reaching the *Reader's Digest*, holding it against the pocket with the pistol. Saying, "Should warn you, aside from cursing, I've been known to talk to myself, middle of the night."

"Bet you snore too."

"Who told you that?"

"I've seen old . . . I mean seniors. You prefer 'seniors'?"

"Long as you don't go with 'fogies,' 'prunes' or 'bats.' And I guess, then, you know about the gas?"

"*Eww.* Double *eww.*"

Grinning, he showed her where the light switch was, then he said, "Good night," went to the back and drew the curtain. Put the *Reader's Digest* down, the .22 on top of it. His years on the force told him the two men would come looking. Not something that kind would let slide. Fitch thinking he better call Milton in case he did fall asleep.

Funny thing, he was feeling alive, hadn't thought about cancer most of the day. Kind of felt like he was telling it to go to hell and find another sucker.

"And you won't call the cops tomorrow?" Wren called in the dark.

"Me, I'm no fink. Plus, there's the hit-and-run and assault. Be too much explaining."

"I could've got whiplash. Maybe I should call my lawyer." Wren giggled.

He told her to do what her conscience allowed, thinking of that movie with John Wayne, the one where the kid went looking for her father's killer, the kid threatening folks with her lawyer.

Wren called out again, "This place got a . . ."

"A loo?"

"A what?"

"Bathroom, it's the same thing."

"Does it?"

"You're practically in it. That door in front of you. Open it, and the light comes on."

She said she thought that was a cupboard, then he heard her going to look, then saying, "Cool." Asking about a tub.

"You put down the lid, and you got yourself a shower. See it over your head?"

"Place is like a Swiss Army knife."

"Right. Oh, and if you do take a shower, take out the toilet roll first, put it on the counter, otherwise it gets soggy."

Then silence, and he started to drift.

Wren saying, "You ever live in a house?"

"Get some sleep."

"Okay."

A few minutes later, he heard her sawing logs. Fitch smiling in the night, lying awake and waiting on Annie, knowing he was going to get an earful. Then remembering he hadn't dumped the colostomy bag before turning in.

... *chick habit*

Zhang Lee sat across from Park Won-Soon with his hands folded, a teacup in front of him. He listened to this rich businessman spill what befell him, how Park played all night, still jet-lagged when he went up to his room; the only reason the two thugs were able to shove him into his room and rob him. Pointed to the staples from the gash on the side of his head.

Zhang nodded and sipped, unconcerned about the man's physical state.

Park went on, how he'd been winning at the tables, blackjack, poker, craps, laying down the Bamboo Union's cash — winning and getting it all laundered — Park saying he couldn't believe how dumb the two thugs were, busting in his door and stealing from the triad, plus the ten grand Park was up from craps. "Of course, that part of the loss will be my own."

Smiling like he appreciated that, Zhang Lee sipped tea.

Park looked at his cup, saying he wondered why chá tasted like dung in this country, all these mountain streams they boasted about.

Zhang smiled and let this rich bag of wind blow.

"Doctor said I was lucky to come away with a few stitches and no concussion." Pulling back his hair and showing the eight staples along his hairline, the patch of shaved scalp, the flesh bruised and raw. "Eight being the sign of wealth," Park said, fingering the hair back in place.

"You went to a hospital?"

"I told the intake nurse I took a tumble, mixing Canadian Club with concrete stairs. Hit my head on the railing and tumbled down a flight." Meaning there was no police report.

Zhang nodded and sipped.

"You'll look for them?" Park said.

Zhang shrugged.

"To get it back." Park looked at him like it had been Zhang who got hit on the head.

"I have you," Zhang said. The cash Park transferred had gone through. This Korean wáng bā dàn trying to get it back, thinking he would just walk away.

"Something like this gets around," Park said, shaking his head. "I come here and get robbed, holding your money. How will that look?"

Zhang looked at him.

"Some may think I was tricked, perhaps set up. Wouldn't be good for business." Park pointed at the stitches again. This quiet man, Zhang Lee, acting more like a Chinese butler than some heavy sent by the Bamboo Union. Park knew the stories of the secret society. Who hadn't grown up hearing of the counterfeiting, trafficking and fraud? Knew how the triad dealt when something didn't go their way. Dismembered hands and feet delivered to loved ones. A head on a pike left in a public square. Stories of entire families vanishing. But Park was a man of position and influence, a Korean businessman at the helm, bringing jobs to hundreds in Jiangsu and Qingdao, their plants making wiring harnesses for the Korean auto giant.

"Tell me of the two men," Zhang Lee said, his hands around his cup like he was warming his fingers.

"I already told you, they pushed the door in, coming in behind me. I struck like a lion." Making a quick chop with the edge of his hand on the table, tea spilling in both saucers. Park shook his finger, saying, "Taught the first one about attacking Park . . ." Then the one finger was four fingers, Park slashing the knife hand through the air.

"Yes, a lion, you said that." Zhang sounding bored. "Yet you were robbed."

"It was the second man . . ." Park narrowed his eyes, not liking the way this errand boy was speaking to him. "A weasel getting behind me as I dealt with the first."

"But they took your money."

"Hit me with something, a gun, I think."

"You know them if you see them again?"

"I see them again, I will get your money back."

"It's how you see it, as my money?" It was the first time Zhang smiled, just a little.

"It belongs to your people, yes. I expect mine to be returned. In good faith, of course."

"Or you go and run your mouth?"

Park drew a long breath, saying, "I understand about wins and losses, my friend, in fact, better than you. I made the transfer, and you handed me the cash. The cash they took. Look, I want no hard feelings here, but that's how I see it, how it is." And he started to rise.

"Sit." Zhang set the cup down.

Park hesitated, sighed like he was bothered, but he sat. "It's the way I just told you: two men came off the elevator and followed me." Park made the same hand strike at the air. "If not for the years of shadowboxing — inside cloud, then hammer." Making a blocking move, snapping a backfist toward the smaller man with his teacup.

Zhang didn't flinch, saying, "They use names?"

"You understand, it happened in seconds. They came through the door. No names, no words. Just the attack, and the man striking me from behind."

"That tells me nothing."

"The one I hit was big. Guǐ lǎo with a pig's face and short yellow hair. The other one was darker-skinned maybe, from one of those hot places."

Zhang looked at him.

"Look, Zhang, I'm sorry about the money. I lost ten thousand of my own . . ." Park shrugged. "In the game there are three things: the rules, the stakes and knowing when to quit." He put up his palms, like this tea drinker could think what he wanted. Like what could he do about it. Leaning forward, he said, "And how do you know one of your own isn't behind it? The ones who knew about the money."

« « «

Pushing the cup farther aside, Zhang met his look and held it.

Unaffected, Park said, "The hospital doctor advised bed rest." Pointing at the staples again. "Told me to wait a few days before flying home. But I'm on the next flight home and sleeping all the way. When I get there, the money will be transferred back, and I will not think of this again."

Zhang kept looking, finally saying, "You used your key card?"

Park frowned and said, "What?"

"When you went to your room, you used the key card."

"Of course."

"And the door has spring hinges, closes on its own."

"Meaning?"

"Meaning it closes and locks, right behind you."

"Yes."

"Yet the two men got in."

"Must have seen me in the casino, saw how I beat the dealer. And they followed me up, right behind me as you say."

"Yet you didn't see them?"

"The jet lag . . ."

"Who was she, the woman?" Zhang looked and waited. There was always a woman, and one who set this fool up. Park just too arrogant to see it.

Park slapped down a palm, played at being tired of the interrogation. Giving back Zhang's burning look. "You know I'm a married man."

The red-haired bartender looked over.

Sending a polite smile, Zhang gave a wave of the hand, waited till the man went back to taking stock. Then he said, "Who is she?"

Park sighed again. "A night of winning, a few drinks, and yes, okay, there was a woman. She watched me raking the chips. Told me she liked a winner, asked if I cared for a drink."

"A jì nǔ."

Looking indignant, Park said, "It wasn't like that."

"She played you, let you show off, let you take her to your room. Saw the money you were showing off, and let you go in first, then she flipped the lock, put something in the door and left it open."

Park acted aggrieved, but a little doubt was slipping in. Finally he puffed air, saying, "Are you married, Zhang?"

Zhang just looked at him.

"Then you can't know. All your life with the same woman . . ."

"You paid her, this jì nǔ."

Park glanced down and gave a nod.

"And the two men, smarter than you, they paid her too." Zhang wasn't so meek now, his eyes burning into Park's.

"Fine, forget the money, but I'm going home."

Zhang Lee shook his head. That wasn't going to happen either. Putting both wrists on the edge of the table, saying, "Let me see it."

"What?"

"Your cloud and your hammer." Zhang leaned his chin forward. "Hit me."

Park got a bewildered look.

"Let me see it."

"Why would I?" Park looked around the bar, couldn't believe it.

"Do it."

Park shook his head like, *this is ludicrous.*

"Hit me and we forget about the money."

"The hundred grand?"

"All of it. Now, let's see it, your cloud, your hammer . . ." Giving him disrespect.

Park grinned like the man had to be joking.

Zhang struck Park in the mouth.

Park's eyes went wild, hadn't seen the man's hand move, going from disbelief to anger.

Zhang set his wrists on the table edge again. Saying, "Now."

"I hit you, then I'll have to deal with yo—"

Zhang's hand shot out again, fingers spearing Park's windpipe.

Park's hand went to his throat. Gagging. Feeling like he couldn't breathe.

The bartender looked over again.

Raising his empty cup, Zhang signaled for more tea. Waited till the bartender turned and moved off. Saying to Park, "One more try." He put his hands in his lap, closed his eyes this time and counted to three. "Yī . . . èr . . . sān . . . " Opened them to Park shaking his head, one hand still at his throat. The anger was there, but the man did nothing.

Zhang nodded and said, "The name the woman gave you."

Collecting himself, Park cleared his throat, his voice weak. "Called herself Valentina."

Zhang nodded, told Park he was going to stay, like he was talking to a dog. Then he went to the bar, two widescreens playing tennis matches. Taking a fifty from his wallet, he folded it on the length and waited for the bartender to come from the back with his tea. Holding the bill between two fingers, letting him see it, he asked, "I want Valentina."

When he returned to the table, he said, "You'll stay and point her out."

A different Park now. Nodding.

"Understand this, the money belongs to you, but also to your wife, your father, your mother, your two sons." Zhang put up a hand and held it flat.

Park flinched.

"And twenty-five thousand more will be in my hand."

Park looked at him confused.

"My fee." No need to threaten this beaten dog, give him a choice of which son he wanted to give up. "By the end of the day."

Park swallowed, then nodded.

Zhang seeing the pale mark on the wrist where Park's watch had been, taking a sip from his cup, he got up, went past the seats, heading toward the same bank of elevators and saying, "There's a cash machine in the lobby."

Following him, Park said the maximum was five hundred from those machines.

"Enough to cover expenses." Zhang took his sleeve and walked him to the lobby. "I'll get you the details, you can transfer the rest."

Park made the cash withdrawal and handed it to him, giving a bow.

"And your key card."

"My room?"

"My room. Don't want you here, but nearby, waiting on my call." Zhang watched Park dig the key card from his pocket, handing it over. His former suite, the one with the mini-bar and the pay-per-view.

"Where nearby?"

Zhang shrugged, guessing this captain of industry would stop at the front desk, ask for the closest motel, leaving him to hope some place had an available room.

. . . fender bending

T he green light showed on the charger, and he took his cell and quietly walked by her. Fitch could tell by her breathing she was asleep. Stepping from the RV, the cardboard taped over the busted window, he moved to the walkway, getting out of earshot. The night breeze coming in off the harbor.

He punched in the number, Fitch looking over the field at the shape of the old Dodge, the light on inside. Could see the silhouette of Minkie's head at the window, sitting and likely reading with their sausage dog, Bullitt, warming her feet. Milton picked up on the first ring, the man afflicted with insomnia, something that had come on strong with the declining years.

"Hey, Fitch, how'd it go, you survive the quacks?"

"Matter of fact, the man gave me a clean bill," he lied.

"Well, good on you. Hold on, let me step outside." Milton saying something about the reception in this tin can, Fitch knowing Minkie didn't like when anyone called at this hour. Fitch heard some muffled sounds, then scraping. Seeing Milton step out of the van across the field, giving him a wave.

He waved back.

Milton saying, "Like I said, you hit the big seven-O, and all bets are off. Not even sure why I go back."

Fitch keeping his appointments because he promised Annie he would. Just never agreed to any chemo, but knowing how she'd feel about it.

Milton going on, "My quack's got me schlucking pills like I'm his bread and butter, the business of sick. A man our age walks in, forget the liver spots, these guys see dollar signs. Pays for their country club."

Fitch betting he was right.

"You go in, get met by that antiseptic air over the smell of death."

"Jeez, you trying to cheer me up, Milt?"

"Just gets me wound up. Just to look at that woman behind the desk, the charm of the grim reaper. Got her sickle right under the desk." Milton was on a roll, no wonder he didn't sleep much, saying, "Minkie's been hounding me to go for my annual: blood pressure, prostate, colon, oil change, the whole shebang. Kee-reist." Chuckling, then lowering his voice. "But I guess that's not why you called."

Fitch watched Milton on the clock pace out front of his extended van. Could see Minkie go to the door, call out to her old man, wondering why on earth Fitch was calling at this hour. Putting up her arm like a wave, Fitch guessing her middle finger was up, just couldn't see it from this distance.

Milton stepped a few more feet away from her, saying, "Anyway, you called me . . ."

"I need a favor." Fitch giving the short strokes, about the two guys at the Potlatch, trying to grab the kid out behind the place.

"The hell did you do?"

"Left my meatloaf." Told about taking the PAM from Dell, and following them out. "Sprayed the one guy in the eyes, got the girl in my rig, arm-dragged the other one across the gravel. Backed into their Ford, broadside, and crunched it like a tin can."

"Goddamn, Fitch. Are you shitting me?"

"Not a bit."

Fitch watching him walk farther from his van, then going back and forth on the sidewalk, Milton saying, "You've got to call the cops, Fitch. Hang up and do it now. Tell them you mixed up your meds. Jesus . . ."

"Be looking at reckless endangerment, assault. May as well hold out my wrists when they come flashing up."

"Jesus, man, a colostomy bag hooked to your bowels, and you walk with a stick . . . Go with Alzheimer's, temporary insanity, blame the fucking meatloaf. Say you blacked out. For a second, you were in Kansas with Dorothy and Toto."

"And . . . the kid's here, in the Brave." From a hundred yards, he watched Milton throw his hands up.

"Oh, my God."

"Can't just put her out on the street."

"Add kidnapping to the list, why the hell not?"

Fitch had to laugh at that.

"You think I'm kidding?" Milton said, "Look, I got this guy we can call, a lawyer. Name's Beauchamp. Old bugger's semi-retired and lives on one of the islands. The kind of case'll make his mouth water." Then Milton was asking about the Brave.

"Old girl held up."

"Come on, Fitch, the two guys already called the law. Their word against yours. You got to know that. From the sounds, their ride's a wreck and the one guy's blind."

"Not the type to call it in."

"You call your insurance, they'll want a police report."

"Dinged the back end a bit, lost a taillight. Bumper's cracked and twisted the ladder. With my deductible, I'll take care of it myself."

Milton was quiet a moment, then said, "You want me keeping a watch, that it? Figure they'll come looking."

"Something like that."

"Well, geez Louise."

Fitch heard Minkie calling Milton. Couldn't tell if her voice was coming through the phone or carried over the field. She had a voice like that, the kind that could shatter glass.

Milton stepped farther into the field, whispering, "You drink warm milk, Fitch. You set your teeth in a glass, and you poop in a bag. I'm telling you, you plead insanity."

"Just need you keeping an eye, Milt."

"You know I will, goddamn it, and probably know I'm gonna ask if you still got that old .22?"

"Come on, Milt, it's the wiener dog of handguns."

"Goddamn it." Milton turned and stepped back to his van, sounding resigned, told Fitch to go to sleep and be with Annie. In the morning, he'd put the word out. Totally Hitched, Wander Woman and Wanderlust, all of them looking out for each other, giving a heads-up anytime bylaws rolled around with their ticket books, and anytime trouble showed up.

. . . *Fitching*

Fitch pulled the curtain from the front windshield, let the morning light in, saw Milton's Dodge in the same spot across the field.

"Since you mentioned Peachland, I've been thinking about leaving myself, maybe catching a ride to L.A." Wren said.

"It's a nice ride down the coast." He didn't even want to think of this kid hopping a ride with strangers.

"You've done it?"

"Many times."

"How long's it take?"

"Twenty hours straight down the 5, give or take depending on the weather, traffic and the state of me being regular."

"*Eww.*"

"At my age, pit stops are a fact of life." Fitch having to go in and dump the bag.

"And you just pull over and sleep in this?"

"And avoid the Motel 6 crawlies." Fitch smiled, thinking what Homeland Security would do to him, sneaking a minor across an international border. Just drive up to the

Peace Arch with the kid on the passenger seat. An old man with a colostomy bag, and a runaway probably with fake ID. Fitch grinning, thinking what the heck, he could cheat any sentence a judge could hand down. Not enough sand left in his hourglass to serve the time. According to Russell, he'd be gone to glory long before the arraignment.

Telling Wren, "On a good run I pushed it to Black Butte without a pit stop, the other side of Oregon."

Oregon wasn't on her radar, Wren wanting to know about Hollywood and palms, the Santa Monica Pier, Toontown, Thunder Mountain and Tomorrowland. She and her mom had talked of staying at the Disneyland Hotel. Fitch seeing in her eyes, that someday was never going to happen.

Then she was steering around her own funk, asking about his daughter, and he told her Carolyn had a baby on the way. The woman a widow at thirty-five.

"That's awful."

"Yeah, a damn shame."

Pointing a finger, Wren said she felt bad about the widow part, but that just cost him another quarter, assuring, "It's for your own good."

"I know, your mom told you that."

"Uh huh."

"You know I'm a pensioner, you understand about that?"

"Then don't swear."

"Still, I think you're hustling me." He made a show of sighing like he gave up, then asked if he could write her a check.

She was shaking her head, smiling, then looking thoughtful. "When are you going to Peachland?"

"Got a few things to work out first."

"Something to do with you road-raging those guys?"

"And saving your tukhus. I can say that, right?"

"I'll let it slide."

"Wasn't the only curve ball thrown my way lately." Surprised again he hadn't thought much about the cancer since leaving Russell's office.

"Okay, let's make it a dime, and call it a senior discount."

"I don't want your pity."

"Well, you did save me. That's worth something."

"Just make it a quarter for Chri—" Fitch changing it to "Christmas."

"Almost."

"I'm living on the edge here."

"It'll do you good."

"I kicked smoking once; it wasn't this tough. And hey, who gets the money? You?"

"The pot. You swear enough and hey, we'll go for meat-loaf. Already up to two-fifty so far." Eating her cereal, she said the Brave didn't seem so cramped anymore.

"Yeah, it grows on you."

"So, tell me about L.A.?"

"You mean what it's like?"

"Uh huh."

"Hot, with smog." He thought about it, saying, "Only thing green's the golf course."

"Thought you liked it?"

"Yeah, I love it."

"You see any movie stars?"

"Oh sure. Saw Eddie Albert in a mall, Ernie Borgnine after a Dodgers game, pretty sure Kim Novak in shades and a straw hat, shopping Melrose."

"I mean anybody I'd know?" She squinted at him.

"How about Paul Newman?"

"The popcorn guy?"

"Before he got into food. *Cool Hand Luke, Butch Cassidy.*" None of it registered.

"And they got lots of sunshine and beaches, right?"

"More than they need. If you go, pack the Hawaiian Tropic, and get the large size." Fitch wanting to say, along with pepper spray. Fifteen and the kid was thinking of L.A. — didn't know a soul and had no idea about the place, a city with teeth. Knowing if she was going, he couldn't stop her, not this kid. Then thinking what Carolyn was going to say when he showed up with a kid — likely something about him picking up strays. Maybe he'd preempt it, saying something like, "Hey, darling, on the way here, look what I found." Already knowing he'd be taking her with him. Looking at her, wondering if this kid had been playing him, asking her if she had a passport.

"I got ID. And it's pretty good."

"By pretty good, you mean fake?"

She smirked.

"You ever hear of Homeland Security?" He shook his head.

"I'm good at hiding in small spaces."

"That's how you got in trouble in the first place. Was hoping you gave that up."

"Wouldn't get in with anybody who smoked. It was the coughing that gave me away."

"Right." Wasn't that long ago when he drove up, the U.S. gatekeepers at the Peace Arch asking the purpose of his visit, and how long he planned to stay. Showed them his driver's license and got waved through. That last crossing, they pulled his Winnebago over, two of the Homeland gestapo searching the RV like he was hiding anthrax and a squad of al-Qaeda. Two hours and a million questions later they let him cross. Could imagine this runaway going to the crossing, with her fake ID and no parental consent letter.

"Good news is you don't need a passport for Peachland."

"That mean I can go?"

"I have a choice?" He smiled at her.

"You're the best."

"Any idea of the jail time I'm racking up?"

"Well, I'm no fink either."

"Sure you haven't done time?" Fitch said.

"I've been in two foster homes." Her look said, yeah, she'd done time.

"Well, before any of that, this old girl needs some looking at." And Fitch had to get his pension and old age checks, and there were people to see, ones who deserved a goodbye.

"How about those two men?"

"Well, if they're smart, they'll be long gone."

"They look that way to you, smart?" She made a face.

... *old school*

Shaking the box of Weetabix, looking inside, Fitch needed to drive to Walmart, stock up and get a few things for the road.

"Oh, I should mention, I can help with the driving. My mom showed me." Wren breaking the cereal with her spoon.

"This ID you have, it a valid driver's license by chance?"

"You worry too much."

Fitch glanced out the windshield, Wander Woman moving her camper to a new spot.

"So your daughter in Peachland . . ."

"Carolyn."

"Right, Carolyn. How did she get . . ." She made a hand gesture at her belly.

"Pregnant?"

"Yeah."

"The usual way. Now, I'm guessing here."

"But her husband passed away . . ."

He'd been wondering that himself, his son-in-law Paul gone nearly two years now. "Started out as bacterial pneumonia

167

before complications set in, then the quick decline. Cashed it in at forty-two."

"Guess that's a good age," she said.

He looked at her. "Forty-two?"

"You know I'm fifteen, right?" Looking out the window, she said, "My mom was forty-six."

He let it sink in, knowing she was a minor in spite of the ID, but didn't know about her mom, saying, "Real shame about your mom. Looking at you, I can tell she was something." Fitch feeling bad, wondering about her dad, but not going to ask right then. He looked out the front, watching Wander Woman step from her camper, smiling his way and waving. Fitch waving back.

"She looks nice," Wren said, looking at him like she was guessing they were more than fellow boondockers.

"Name's Monica, and we're just friends." Almost said "Christ" again. Wondering how this kid got so savvy, betting if she went to church on Sundays, she'd be leading the sermon.

"Tell me about this friend." Wren was grinning, looking at her out the window.

"What's to tell?"

"Made me think of my friend Maude, wondering what she'd make of you."

"Me?"

"Could be you'd get along."

"What makes you think I want to get along?"

"I don't know, call it a hunch."

"You ask me, you're overthinking things," Fitch told her. Then he took his cell, ducked the conversation by dialing Milton, asking for one more favor. Wanting to know if Wren could watch his TV while he made a shopping run. Wanted to keep her out of sight in case the two creeps came around.

She rolled her eyes.

Fitch warning his buddy to watch his language, or he'd up end in the poor house. When he hung up, he said, "You're gonna love these folks."

"Love they got a TV."

"And a wiener dog."

"Cool. Except I might be allergic."

"To dogs?"

"Uh huh."

"Thing's the size of a guinea pig." Fitch showing with his hands.

She told about the couple in Stanley Park, and their dog, and the woman with the Boston terrier, no adverse reaction to either one.

"Well, there you go then."

"That who you called last night when you figured I was asleep?" she said.

The kid didn't miss a trick. Fitch nodded and said, "And you could have said something about the snoring." He tapped the water jug's spigot, measured a couple cups' worth and poured it. Pressed the button and waited for the machine to heat up, then inserted a capsule.

Wren saying, "Never heard that, just you talking to yourself. Must've slept right through it."

"Wasn't talking about me." Pointing at her, pulling down the table, putting the box of cereal on it, setting out a couple of bowls.

"Tell me you're joking," she said. "I don't snore."

The girl sounded like a propeller, but he said, "Yeah, I'm an old kidder."

"Well, quit it, that's mean."

He got the last banana from the fruit bowl.

"You ever eat anything fun in the morning, no offense?" Looking at the box.

He frowned, opened the last packet and put a Weetabix in each bowl.

She said no thanks to the banana, watched him slice off a bruised spot, then slice half with a bread knife, plopping pieces into his bowl.

She took a spoon to the dry cereal, and took a bite.

"Needs some milk," he said.

"And some flavor."

"It's what we call honest cereal."

"Who's we?"

"The ones who know what's good for you. Flavor comes from the banana. It's how it works." He poured her a cup, ejected the capsule and fixed himself one.

"Food can be fun, you know?" She took a sugar cube and crushed it over the cereal.

"So what's your idea of cereal?"

"Well, I just went through a Cocoa Puffs stage — you know, the one with the cuckoo bird. Loved it with chocolate milk . . . Lucky Charms before that."

"Snap, crackle, pop, right?"

"That's Rice Krispies. Lucky Charms are magically delicious." She tried her coffee, thanked him and nodded her approval.

"Comes with a free toy inside, right?"

"Maybe back in the stone age. These days it's likely to be a code for an online game or something, if anything at all."

"A what?"

"Take too long to explain it." Looking at the Weetabix box, she said, "What do you get in this?"

"You get regular."

"*Eww.*"

And the two of them were laughing.

The knock at the door had them both jumping, Fitch getting up, resisted going for the .22 under the *Reader's Digest* by his bedside.

Milton was standing at his door, looking at the cardboard where the window should be.

"Scared the bejesus out of me," Fitch said, holding the door and letting him in.

Wren called from the table, "That's a quarter."

Fitch rolled his eyes, told Milton they were just finishing up breakfast, then he brought him back and introduced them.

« « «

One thing was sure, the sooner they got on the road, the better. He'd go use the ATM this one time and empty his savings. Any luck, the bumper wasn't cracked, and the boys at Norseman's could take off the twisted roof ladder and get him on the road pronto. No time to order up a taillight assembly for a '76 Winnebago, but they could rig something temporary.

Driving to Walmart, Fitch didn't feel any wobble in the steering column now. And the grinding sound was gone. He'd cranked his wheels and caught the big Ford broadside with the rear corner on his driver's side, minimizing his own damage.

Calling Marty at Norseman's, he was told next week at the earliest, no way they could see him sooner. Fitch would have to take his chances. Stick to the posted limit, and with a good tailwind, the old girl would make the four-hour run. Smiling, thinking of the kid offering to chip in for gas and help with the driving. Even knew an apprentice mechanic in Richmond who could help them out. Fitch told her, "You're a guest, and guests don't work, and they don't pay."

Yeah, it was crazy, driving to Peachland with a runaway, but the kid had a way of tugging at the old heartstrings, her and that swear jar and fake ID. Under the stolen fur jacket there was a good heart. And what else could he do? Wasn't going to turn her loose or call it in. Fitch with little faith in the system and less with life on the street for runaway teens. Finding a spot to park out behind the mall, he felt a stab in his chest, saying, "Go fuck yourself." Then he fished in a pocket for a quarter and flipped it onto the passenger seat, guessing he better get a jar, make it a large one. When the wave of pain passed, he took his crutch and got out. Started to put the key in the lock, looked at the taped-up window, and forgot about it.

. . . *smoggers and wheezers*

A shame about the Expedition, Angel saying the car ring wouldn't take it damaged. Cooder had rigged the sliding door with a bungee, but the thing didn't close right. Too hot to hang on to, they had to dump it. Cooder leaving it a block east of Lower Lonsdale. Five hundred bucks down the toilet.

Put the transmitter in his jacket pocket and walked up Lonsdale. Passed on a Volvo wagon, put his eyes on a Durango with its flashers on, but the guy came back too soon, then he spotted an Alfa Romeo pulling down a side street, stopping behind a bakery. It wasn't on the list of cars the garage was after, but what the hell, it looked sharp. And the hipster getting out with his powder-blue scarf around his neck, and one of those douche hats and patent shoes with no socks, that guy was begging for it. Turning, the guy aimed his fob and went in the bakery's back door. Cooder trapping the signal from the street.

Looking around, he got in, backed up and drove off, adjusting the seat and mirrors. Checked the fuel gauge, the needle on half. Pressed play on the CD and got some cool jazz. Rolling along Marine, he pulled in the south lot of Cap Mall, found a spot to park. A two-bit security guard out front of the liquor store sized him up like he was on surveillance. Going past a produce market and turning down another wide hall, looking for the old geezer on his stick, a silver head and splotches on his face, thinking they called them liver spots. A cluster of oldsters perched on stools, playing chess out front of Orange Julius. Cooder scanned the faces. Any heads that weren't gray were bald, walkers and mobility scooters all over the place. A daytime hangout for the fossils. The only thing missing was bingo. But none of them were his guy.

His cell gave that air-raid tone, a Middle Eastern couple glancing his way as they passed. Looking at the caller ID, he said, "Christ," answered the call and said, "Well, there you are, Muff." Trying to sound happy to hear her voice.

"Said you were coming over. Made my mac and cheese and everything. Turning into a goddamn clump."

"Yeah, sorry, something's come up."

"You're such a dick."

Caught himself from calling her a cunt. "When did we agree to lunch?"

"You never hear a word."

"Said you had shit to process, and I get that. Told me to figure where I want to be."

"And where's that?"

"Exactly what I been thinking about." Cooder not sure if crying or yelling came next — could go either way.

"I counted on you, Cooder, was hoping you'd accept some responsibility. Guess I was wrong."

The guilt trip.

Before he could say anything more, she was gone.

Cooder stood looking at his phone, finally let go his grip, no point trying to crush it. Dropping it in his pocket, he walked through this mall of stale air and artificial daylight, this place depressing the hell out of him. Reminded himself why he was there, looking for that old fuck with the walking stick — and God pity the old man when he caught up with him.

The big-box store was a sea of tasteless fake leather and home-furnishing knockoffs and markdowns, a showroom the size of a ball park, where the Sears had once been. A kitsch jewelry exchange manned by a Middle Eastern dude giving him a suspicious look, then a kiosk selling lotto cards. Get your kicks fixed at Sal the Cobbler's — Sal also cutting keys. Next to the shoes was an off-the-rack menswear offering any three-piece on the rack, a steal for a hundred and fifty, taxes in. Cooder thinking, "Give me chinos and a crewneck any day, let a man breathe."

Then thinking what to do with Tracy, the girl all thankful to the Lord for the blessed event, and Cooder cursing Christ for a faulty rubber. Always hated the way little kids cried day and night, so fucking needy and unreasonable. Now Tracy was getting like that too.

His shoulder ached from being arm-dragged and smacked down by that camper. He retraced his steps to the south end of the mall. A salesman called from a door, said he had the best phone plans and deals on airtime in the Lower Mainland. Another guy, could be his twin, at the counter leaning on an elbow, playing with his own phone. Minimum wage, nothing to do, and no daylight. Cooder waved them off and kept walking.

The old boys playing chess at the food court looked like the only airtime they gave a shit about came from an oxygen tank. Looking over the faces again — none of them the crazy old man. The Walmart greeter studied him in passing, Cooder saying, "Ain't you supposed to be smiling?"

The guy glanced at Cooder, rubbing his middle finger against his cheek.

"There you go." Laughing, he went by Vacay's Luggage having a must-go sale, in case this fucking mall depressed the hell out of him enough, and he felt the need to skip town. Like he did now.

The after-school crowd was filtering in the automatic doors, groups of kids with backpacks filling up the tables, oblivious of everyone else, the chess players starting to pack it up. One tall kid coming up and asking if Cooder'd get him a six of Coors. "Sure, kid." Taking the kid's money, turning into the liquor store, Cooder snapped up a six of Bud, paid, then ignored the kid on his way out, and went and found the Alfa Romeo.

Squinting into the late-afternoon sun, he was careful approaching the car in case it had been staked out. Feeling right, he switched the device and got in, set the Bud on the opposite seat and drove out of there. When Angel got back from dealing with the chick, Valentina, they'd drop this ride off at the chop shop by the Auto Mall.

Valentina had been calling Angel's number all day, leaving pissed-off messages. Finally saying she had something else, something bigger, and told him not to be such a two-bit chump. Angel saying to Cooder, "What could it hurt, hear her out?"

Cooder told him he had a bad feeling. Angel saying he worried too much and ought to learn who to trust, then he showered, dressed, slapped on the aftershave and drove off in his 'Stang, took half the money in his army surplus duffel. Left Cooder to dump the Expedition.

Turning out to be a good earning day, in spite of losing out on the Expedition, getting hit by a guy half his size, then by another guy twice his age.

Had a moment when he felt like calling Tracy and giving her back some of her own shit, tell her he came to his senses, also came into some real money, knock her from her moral high ground. The bitch slapping him like that in Taco Bell, then hanging up on him today.

Life was too short for bimbos like that. Plus, in the sack, he had to do the work, her enthusiasm barely above a distraction. Yeah, he was better off without her, deciding not to call back.

Driving out of the lot, he felt superior to a chick for the first time in his life, popped the first can, sipping that nice cold beer. Man, his shoulder hurt, elbows and knees scraped from getting tossed, and had a good pair of chinos ripped.

The day starting with the Asian guy pulling that Jackie Chan crap. His leg and foot hurting too, the nail of his big toe split down the middle. Back at Angel's, he'd tugged off the sock and looked at the mess. Wrapped a Band-Aid around it. Little twerp half his size spearing him in his eyes and stomping on his foot. Same day the old man arm-dragged him, his Happy Camper smacking up the Expedition, costing him five hundred bucks. Not moves they taught at the old folks' center.

Nothing like that happened when he was a fourth-line enforcer on the ice. Everybody knew who he was and why he was there. His number got called, and he stalked, got opposing players off their game, provoking with his hips and putting his stick in a face, getting them to drop the gloves. That's when he came alive — doing what he was born to do. Grabbed a handful of jersey and flailed like a trip hammer, making a forward bleed, while gaining some respect. Making the seconds count before the refs pulled him off and sent him to the box.

But to his mind, they had squared it with the Asian, left the man bleeding on the rug and took his Canucks bag and cleaned out the wall safe. Cooder's share being more money than he ever made playing hockey, and more than enough to forget the pain. But the old man doing what he did, that left a score to settle.

Mid-afternoon, he kept up the search, rolling the Alfa south of the Auto Mall, the water of the inlet shimmering ahead of him. Turning along Harbourside, looking at a handful of faded eyesores parked around the vacant field. Remembered an article in the *North Shore News* dubbing these homeless on wheels "boondockers." A photo of a gray-haired couple out front of their mobile home, the look of leftover hippies from the time of dropping acid and making free love, wearing headbands and beads. Smogging and wheezing, these mobile wrecks looked like they couldn't limp a dozen miles before a breakdown. Reading the names on the back, but not seeing the one he was looking for.

A hoarding faced south, its rendering of luxury condos to be built on this site. Three-hundred-sixty-degree views and master-planned. Just what this city needed, tossed-up wood-frame construction, another blend of retail and residential living. Meaning another glut of Beemers and Benzes would clog the arteries to the downtown side. Cooder doing his bit to aid urban congestion, stealing cars one at a time, to be sold overseas or broken down for parts. Making five hundred a pop.

Finding a spot, he tucked the Alfa between a couple of Evos, the dark blue putt-putts that rented by the hour, a fleet of them lined along the curb. A faded camper on an old Dodge pickup, an extended van with a tarp over the roof to keep out rain. Wander Woman and other stupid names.

Taking the rest of the six-pack, Cooder got out and looked at people walking their dogs, one old-timer with a squashed face sitting in a fold-up lawn chair on a patch of boulevard grass, facing the view of the city over the water, the light gleaming off skyscraper windows, a SeaBus crossing past the barges and tankers. A seaplane taking off.

Stepping to the walk, he approached the old man from the front, didn't want to startle him into a coronary, nodding to get his attention. Reminded Cooder of one of those Chinese dogs, the kind with all the loose skin. The old man's eyes hardly showing under the folds, the guy like Father Time. Cooder saying, "Got a nice spot picked out, huh, Pops?"

"I know you?" The old man used his hand like a shield, squinting up at him.

"Always heard yours was the friendly generation," Cooder forced a smile, adding, "What my folks told me."

"You lost or something, son?"

"Just being friendly." Cooder lifted the six-pack.

"Free country last time I checked." The old-timer sized him up, his eyes resting on the Bud.

"Yeah, had a free afternoon, off of work, you know. Thought I'd head down, catch some rays, have a cold one and watch some boats."

"You selling something?"

"You can't sell friendly, Pops." Shifting the beer from one hand to the other, he extended his right, saying, "I go by Cooder." Realized his mistake, using his real name, then waging the old guy's short-term recall was probably like Swiss cheese.

"Milton." The old man leaned to shake the hand.

"Bet a beer'd hit the spot, huh, Milt?" Cooder smiling, pulling a can from the plastic ring.

"It cold?"

"Sure, it's cold."

"But hey, if you're trying to sell me something . . ."

"I got nothing to sell, I promise you that." Cooder guessing the well-to-do walking their pedigrees didn't stop and talk to these boondockers. Walking past these oldsters like senility was contagious. He popped the tab on a can, holding it out.

« « «

Milton guessed who the guy was when he stepped from the fancy car parked on the opposite side, but beer was beer, and from across the field, Minkie couldn't get a good look. Plus, the girl Fitch rescued was in his extended van, chatting with Minkie, the two of them getting on like a house on fire. Fitch driving off in his Brave and making a run to the mall, getting some chuck, treating the runaway girl like a house guest. Said he was taking her to Peachland, visit his daughter. Not that he was asked, Milton telling him what he thought of the idea, how he ought to call Child Services. Not sure what got into his old friend.

Just knew he was going to miss him, but right now, he was hoping the kid was smart enough to stay indoors. And that Fitch wasn't hurrying back.

Setting down the stringer of beer cans, Cooder stuck a hand in his pocket and said he was looking for a pal. "Maybe you know him."

"This pal got a name?"

"Just a guy I ran into at the place I was having lunch. Funny, didn't catch the name. Sure an interesting fellow though. Hair gone gray, thin on top, maybe about seventy or so, walks with a stick, pants pulled up to here." Cooder smiled.

"Man, you just described half the North Shore." Milton grinned, tipping up the can, "Could be talking about me."

"He's got an old camper, stripes on the side. Happy Camper on the spare tire cover, hanging off the back. Yellow letters, or could be white. And you know, swishy . . ."

"Like a script?" Milton took a sip, said the temperature was just right. Minkie was sure to smell it on his breath, but nothing she could do to stop him after the fact.

"Yeah, like script, I guess. A cream-colored rig, maybe one time it was white." The big man shifted his eyes around, then looked at him, Milton smiling, betting this guy was thinking, cream-colored like the color of his old teeth.

Milton's look said it wasn't ringing any bells.

Cooder frowned, then took another stab. "Could have a kid with him, a girl."

"Like a niece or granddaughter?"

"Something like that." Cooder showed her height with his hand. "Skinny kid about yea high, brown hair, straight and long. Could be she runs track."

"Runs track?" Milton looked at him, figured this guy couldn't win in the game of life if it was rigged.

"Well, had that look, on account of being skinny, like she could run."

"Sure." Milton counted on his fingers. "Let's see, we got an old guy, pants up to here, a Happy Camper in white, and a skinny kid that runs track."

"Right."

"So this Happy Camper, how many axles we talking?" Milton having fun now.

"Think I'd know that, how many axles?" The guy named Cooder forced a smile, stretching his mouth tight. Milton ventured the man was recalling Fitch's Brave rushing backwards. This being the guy he dragged and threw to the gravel. Fitch spraying fire at his buddy's face. Then bucking their SUV into the cinder blocks out back of the Potlatch.

All before the meatloaf got cold. Yeah, Milton sure would have loved to see it.

"How's your beer?"

Milton let go a silent burp, saying, "Bud's the crown jewel of brews, as long as it's cold, which it is. Cheers." Sipping more.

"So you help me out or not, Milt?"

Pretending to mull it over, Milton took another pull and gurked up wind, loud this time, saying, "When you say rig, you mean a camper or an RV?"

"There a difference?"

"Well, one you pull, the other you don't."

"Then the kind you don't. An all-in-one. And the one I'm talking about's got stripes, orange maybe." The big man tossed his empty on the grass and popped another can for himself.

"An RV then."

"Right." Took a big swallow, foam going down the side of his lips. Sending his tongue after it, Cooder said, "Like I said, two of us met at lunch, this place on Pemberton —"

"The Potlatch?"

"That's it, burgers are aces. Guess you know it?"

"Good, but a bit pricey for the pension set."

"So the two of us got talking table to table, you know. Told me he was camped down here. Said if I had the time, come and look him up."

Man, this guy was dumb. Likely pegged Milton for adult diapers, and wouldn't believe Fitch had been a sergeant major with the RCMP, twice decorated. The guy who took him and his buddy out with a spray can and a Winnebago. Now this dummy was back for more.

"Something funny?"

"Just the gas . . . been a while since I had one of these." Milton looking fondly at the can, taking a careful sip.

"Yeah, thought I'd catch up, hear more of his stories. And this guy had plenty of them." The big man looked around the vacant lot again. "Reminded me of my old man, you know?"

"Well, if it's stories you want . . ."

"Sure you got some good ones too, and maybe another time . . . think I'll give the food court another shot."

"Best warn you, the food's low and the prices high. The sub place is okay, but the Thai Tanic joint dishes up mostly rice," Milton warned.

"Keep it in mind."

"Some of the Kiwanis boys play chess up there — socialize and keep the wits sharp. Could ask there, maybe they can help." Knowing Fitch would have entered Walmart from the other side, away from the food court, and likely to leave the same way.

Cooder said he'd do that, reaching and peeling another can off the rings, considering it. "You up for one more?" Holding it out.

"Well, now . . ." Bribed with beer. Milton nodded thanks, taking the last swallow, handing back the empty and taking the new one, guessing this guy pegged him for knowing more than he was giving up, hoping the beer would loosen him up.

Popping another one himself, Cooder looked across the field, then out over the water.

Adjusting himself through the checked trousers, Milton muttered something about his goddamn scrotum becoming a goddamn slingshot. Sipping and knowing he'd be peeing Niagara in about ten minutes, the porta-potty the closest toilet. At his age, you had to have eyes on the closest toilet, or it could be trouble. He said, "You ever play?"

"Pocket pool?" Cooder grinned.

"Chess."

"Me? Naw."

"More a pinochle man myself," Milton said.

"That right?" Cooder spotted something moving out on one of the chained logs, pointed his can at it.

"A harbor seal," Milton said. "Ought to see them in the summer, sometimes forty, fifty of them sunning and barking."

"Got told fishermen used to shoot them."

"The wife thinks they're cute."

Cooder looked at him, saying, "You're not going to help me out, are you?"

"Told you what I know, Cood." Milton gave a shrug.

Cooder's look clouded over, and Milton guessed he ought to be afraid of this guy. Scratching behind an ear, he looked at his fingernails like maybe some scalp had scraped off. Saying, "Look, a lot of folks come and go, but Happy Camper . . ." He shook his head, like it wasn't ringing a bell. Then he tapped his temple, like a thought just arrived. "There's this website, set up like a bulletin board for boon-dockers. Tells the best spots, where we won't get harassed and run off." Milton rhyming off the web address.

"Yeah, maybe I'll give it a google." Cooder looked like he was ready to go, then said, "You know, Milt, I think maybe you been jerking my chain." Tucking the last can under his arm, Cooder crushed his empty and bounced it off Milton's chest, some foam landing on his shirt.

"Beer's making you hostile, son," Milton said, watching him snap the tab of the new can, looked like he wished it was Milton's neck. Tempted to point out the trash can a dozen steps away, Milton supposed he'd pushed his luck far enough. This guy not right in the head. But he'd given Fitch enough time to go shopping, guessed he'd be heading back soon.

"Used to go camping, when I was a kid on family trips," Cooder said, making a show of enjoying his beer. "Pitched a tent and went and fetched kindling. Toasted marshmallows, got a stringer of perch, jacket potatoes in the coals, corn on the cob. Singing around the fire. Yeah, that's camping. Don't know what this is."

"Well, we've got no perch, and you even try to light a fire down here . . ." Milton smiled, looked at the SeaBus going wide past a freighter. The *Constellation* paddle steamer all lit up, wheeling past an anchored barge, silhouettes of tourists on its upper deck, the last dinner cruise of the season. "Get to my age, you can forget marshmallows. And the only corn I get's on my feet."

"Good to know." Cooder tipped his can, no idea about dropping his teeth in a glass at night, or getting by popping an assortment of prescription pills and eating strained food. "And I bet you look out for each other, give each other a heads-up when the man with the ticket book comes around. Or anybody else not looking right." Cooder downed the beer and dropped the can on the grass. Took the last one off and tossed away the plastic rings.

Milton pointed at it. "Seagull gets its head in there, good chance it strangles."

"Be one less dump duck shitting up the place then."

"Not into ecology then?"

Cooder started to turn from Milton's patch of heaven.

"You want to leave a number, case I see this Happy Camper?"

"Maybe I'll come back." Cooder stepped toward the Alfa.

Milton thinking he had to go see a man about a dog in the worst way, waiting until the big man drove away. Then he made double time, going for the porta-potty, praying it wasn't occupied.

185

. . . on the clock

One look, and he knew it was her. Didn't need to have
Park Won-Soon point her out. The woman sat at the
bar, model straight, shoulders pulled back, one leg crossed
over the other, the foot dangling a pump and jiggling it like
bait. Zhang Lee watched her from the booth. Started to
understand the five hundred Park had paid her, the man
thinking he was going to get laid, instead getting laid out.

Mid-afternoon and a dozen players were taking a break
from the tables, coming into the lounge for lunch and lube.
Most of the men were solo, all of them stealing looks.

According to Park, she went by Valentina, sitting like
she was unaware of the glances. Sweeping her dark hair
back with a hand. Her face made up, the tight green number
clinging to the curves. Zhang guessed the bartender set a
watered drink in front of her. Recrossing her legs, the dress
hiked up a little more. Perfect skin that said come and get
it, boys.

Zhang pictured how it had played. Valentina setting Park
up, watching him stack chips at blackjack, then at craps,
smiling like she liked a winner. Suggesting they get a drink,

showing him the town, then going to his room, leaving the door open. Stepped out of the way when the thugs muscled in, and watched it happen. Park not able to call the cops, with no way to explain the stolen cash. He let the woman help him into a cab and take him to emergency.

One of the men at the far end of the bar was moving in, tall and wide in the shoulders, about mid-forties and good-looking, heading for the stool next to her. Zhang stepped in front, and the guy gave him a look and said, "Hope you drive better than you walk."

Zhang just looked at him.

The man thought better of doing anything more and turned and went back to his seat, shaking his head, sending Zhang dirty looks. Sitting on the stool next to her, Zhang ordered a single malt neat. The bartender nodded, getting the drink. Images on the big-screen TVs, a soccer match on one, tennis on the other. When his drink came, he took a taste, turned to her and smiled, the woman smiling back, saying to him, "I'm waiting, see what line you come up with." She smiled perfect teeth, taking him in, not hiding that she was doing it.

"Maybe I was hoping you'd go first," Zhang said, finding it easy to smile at her.

"Never tried it."

"Could start by thanking me, saving you from that guy." Zhang looked down the bar at the other guy, the guy still looking over.

"Think I needed saving?"

"He's not your type."

"Ah, and how about you?"

"I'm a whole different story."

» » »

187

Handsome with wide shoulders under the Gucci threads, suggesting some hard hours in the gym. Nikki bet he had the washboard abs. Ten Gs worth of timepiece on his wrist, gold links and the white-gold ring with diamonds that likely cost as much as the watch. A haircut that ran him a hundred bucks easy, teeth whitened by laser, nails done in a salon. Nikki Miller, going by Valentina when she was working, was assessing this one. Saying to him, "The look says out of town, but the voice is local, more or less." Meaning his Asian looks with just a slight accent.

"More people in China learning English than all of North America," he said. The smile did little to soften the eyes.

"Just need to work on your pickup lines." Swiveling his way in her chair, and knowing the way she did it, she could've taught Sharon Stone to cross her legs. "So you're not here for the sights . . ."

"Like the muddy Fraser?" He nicked his head to the window at the brown current.

"Just here to play then." Smiling and sizing him up. He wasn't giving off a vice cop or creep vibe. And he didn't look like he'd flinch when she told him how much. This one might even be fun. She needed something going right after the debacle yesterday morning, the two assholes taking off with her money.

"Not big on games of chance," he said.

"No?"

"I'm more about the sure thing." Still smiling.

"Could be boring."

"Not the way I do it." He offered his hand, introducing himself as Frank.

"Valentina." Nikki took the hand and held it a moment, still not getting a "wrong" vibe. Not the kind to be into some kinky shit he wasn't getting at home, or the rough stuff that would mess up her looks. Yet there was something dangerous, or maybe it was just mysterious. Either way, she had the 9mm Ruger in the handbag, right on the bar top next to the drink with the melting ice. Thought it might come in handy if she caught up to Angel and his louse of a partner, get back what they owed her.

"So, Frank, what do you do when you're not playing?"

"I'm kind of a fixer."

"Yeah, what do you fix?"

"Company sends me when a situation needs smoothing, somebody in need of a fresh perspective, that kind of thing. Mostly I just talk."

"You bring the cool, get everyone to chill." Looking at him, smiling on account he wasn't saying anything.

"You're kinda right." He tried from another angle. "Let's say a guy's looking at a situation the wrong way, I'm the guy who goes in and gives him an adjustment."

"Or maybe it's a her."

"It could be."

"So it's like employee relations?"

"Kind of like that, yeah."

"You realize you just said nothing?" Smiling at him.

Zhang smiling back.

« « «

"You get me talking the fine strokes, I'll just put you to sleep." It was so easy to smile at this woman. God, those eyes — could fall right into them and keep right on tumbling.

"Want to bet?" Leaning close, she let the Chanel do its job. Considered that he could be here about the guy getting robbed yesterday. Then picking up her glass, saying, "So, somebody here need fixing?"

"There is a guy I came to see."

"You're working now?"

"Right now, I'm buying a lady a drink."

"I've got a drink." She jiggled the glass, then knocked it back, eyes staying on his. "But since you offered . . ."

Zhang signaled to the bartender and told him, "Two more, the same way." Slapping back his own, saying, "How about you, you a mystery?"

"I'm more an open book."

"Like to hear the story then. Everybody's got one, right?"

"Still not sure if yours is about work or pleasure."

"Why can't it be both?"

"Guess I'm intrigued then," she said.

The bartender set down the drinks. Zhang waiting till the red-haired guy shuffled off, looking at her, saying, "What else d'you want to know?"

"First, I wondered if there's a badge in your pocket?" Smiling and putting a hand above his knee.

He held his hands wide, smiling at her eyes. "You want to frisk me . . ."

"Might be fun." Her other hand slipped inside his jacket and felt around. "How am I doing, getting warm?"

"More than you know." Letting her do it. His eyes stayed on hers.

"Could get warmer." Whispering a number, she took her hands back. Holding her wrists out, putting them together like she was waiting for him to cuff her.

"You'd just cry entrapment."

"Plus I'm not into handcuffs."

"Not my thing either." He took her hand gently and kissed the top of it, saying, "Mother raised her boy to treat women right."

"Glad you didn't say gentle." Taking her glass, she tapped it to his, saying, "Chin-chin."

Like on cue, the bartender swung by and set down the tab, Zhang reached his wallet and dropped a couple of bills down.

"So, you got a room, Frank?" she whispered.

He got up and reached in a pocket, flashing Park's key card.

Leaning close, she said, "We can take care of the details when we go up, and if you want to tip me after, well, that's up to you." She kissed his ear as her eyes swung around the bar, the guy Zhang had stepped in front of still watching.

Along with every other male in the place. Nobody would remember him, Zhang was sure of that, the two of them walking across the patterned carpet. In her heels, this woman taller than he was. Not sure why that bothered him. Taking his hand, going to the elevators, the same way she had led Park the day before, setting him up to get mugged.

He pressed the floor button, and she eased him to the back wall as the door closed, Zhang watched their mirrored images, the woman drawing against him. Putting his hands on the small of her back, the Chanel filling his head. Her tongue going down his neck as the elevator stopped, Zhang thinking it was pleasure before business this time around.

A maid stood with a cart, on swollen legs in a blue uniform, tired eyes looking at them as the door opened, weary with disinterest. Zhang held the door and Valentina stepped out, the maid bumping the cart in, a stack of towels on top, cleaning supplies muffling the scent of Chanel. The maid nodding a thanks.

Taking Valentina's hand, he walked to the door, pushed her back against it and kissed her as he swiped Park's card, and pushed the door open. Caught the look in her eyes, Valentina realizing too late it was the same suite, the player she set up the day before. He pushed her in and shut the door, switching on the light.

Smiling, looking like she was trying to put it together, backing to the king-sized bed, her hand dipped in her handbag, started to turn to him.

Two steps and he grabbed the Ruger coming out, snapping it from her hand, emptying the shells and tossing the piece to the corner. She started to cry out and his hand caught her throat, cutting off her wind. Twisting her and shoving her to the wall, pinning her against it, his fingers on her windpipe. Saying, "Now, you see, I'm working." Giving her a second, he felt her swallow, pushing her up on her toes. Her eyes full with fear, she tried to bring a knee up between his legs.

Blocking it with his thigh, he waited, letting her realize there was nothing she could do. Then he eased his grip, letting her get some air, saying, "And you know why I'm here?"

She waited, then gave a nod.

And he let go of her throat. "The man's name's Park. He tell you that?"

She nodded again.

"You saw him as a mark, a middle-aged rich guy far from home. Offering him what he's likely not getting from some worn-out shoe who had his kids."

A slight nod.

"Your two buddies come in right behind you and knock him out and rob him. You hang back, call the ambulance, get him stitched up, playing the victim too so you can still show your face here. How am I doing?"

She shrugged, saying, "Part of it."

"I want the money back."

Her eyes were on his, the woman trying to control her fear.

"How this ends depends on you. You understand that?"

And now the tears.

He lifted her chin with a finger, saying, "I'm not playing now, understand? I want to meet your pals."

She hesitated, his finger and thumb like a vice on her windpipe. When she bobbed her head, he eased up again. Letting her know what he could do was worse than anything the two men could dream up.

"Guy's name's Angel." Her voice was rough. She put up a hand, needing a moment, trying to recall the other name. Tears making lines down her cheeks. Drawing more air, saying, "The other one's Cooper, something like that. He's supposed to be the muscle, only he's too dumb for it."

He gave her time, saying, "Where do I find them?"

"Number's on my phone." Nikki looked at her bag on the floor.

Zhang pushed her back onto the bed, reached it and handed it to her. Her legs apart in the tight dress, but this was all business now.

"Already called him and left a hundred messages, the son of a bitch. Let me do the work, then screwed me over." She put a hand in the bag, doing it slow, waiting till he nodded that it was okay, and took out her phone.

"Your line of work, you get paid up front, no?"

"Can't believe I let them rip me off. Guess I'm dumber than they are."

"You're being hard on yourself."

A tap at the door, Nikki looking hopeful.

Zhang leaned closer and told her, "You understand I don't play?" Waited for her to nod, took the phone from her hand, then moved for the door and glanced at the peephole.

The same maid stood at the door with her trolley, wanting to make up the room. No do-not-disturb sign on the door. Looking at Valentina, he fished in a pocket and cracked the door, told the maid to come back, handed her a ten for her troubles, putting on the *Do not disturb*. The maid tucked away the bill, said, "Yes, sir," and pushed her cart along the hall.

Closing the door, Zhang turned back, handed her the phone again. Valentina sat on the bed, a little more composed. She found pen and paper by the nightstand and jotted down Angel's number, handing it to him.

"Could use a drink, how about you?" He stepped to the mini-bar and set a fistful of tiny bottles on top, found a half bottle of bubbly, another of zin, and asked her pleasure. Zhang back to talking like it was a date.

Going for a vodka straight, she downed it in two swallows, saying without being asked, "Think he said something about North Van."

"Give me a picture of this Angel guy?"

"About your height, black hair, longish, losing a bit in the front. His eyes don't line up, and he dresses loud, like he's a wheel, you know? The kind who loves himself." Rolled her eyes. "Told me all about his car, horsepower and header pipes, the kind a guy drives when his manhood's in short supply."

Zhang poured himself a Cutty Sark.

She passed her empty glass back, Zhang offering rum or gin.

Picking the rum, she said, "The one called Cooper shows up in one of those safari hats, supposed to be the muscle. Don't know his story. Like I said, mostly he's dumb." She downed the second drink. "Only time I talked to him was on the phone, the guy taking a message for Angel. You know what he asks me?"

Zhang waited.

"Asks me what he'd get for twenty these days. You believe it? Told him for that he gets the time of day."

"So you got Park to the room, this room."

Nikki looked around, saying, "The little guy put up a fight, and with a . . ." Her hand gesturing, meaning with an erection. "Took the big man by surprise, and would've taken care of him. Was Angel clocking him from behind with a pistol, putting him down."

"This being your plan?"

"Should have been easy, me baiting an out-of-town player, and Angel coming in and pulling his pistol, robbing the guy, maybe doing a Murphy, you know, me playing his old lady, him being beside himself, that kind of thing. Only he insists on bringing his buddy on account Angel's got a problem with his eye, needs his buddy to do the driving. Should have known right there."

"So they come in, rough him up and take the money."

"We all walk out, except they get greedy and rip me off. Half not being enough."

"All of you figuring Asians for easy marks."

"I figure you for rich, the ones coming here to play, nothing to do with being Asian. Look, I read this thing in the paper, called it the Vancouver model. How they can only leave home with a limited amount of cash, making a deal with a triad and picking up all the playing money they want. Have a good time, fly home and nobody's the wiser. Me, I figure some are going to want to play with more than money. Their wives back at home none the wiser."

"And never bothered you where the money's from?"

"Guess I'm as dumb as the one in the hat."

"That what you thought, you see me coming up at the bar, here's another Asian."

"You want to know what it was?"

"Tell me."

Tapping a painted nail at the crystal on his watch, she said, "Figured you for about ten grand worth of Rolex." Pointing at the ring. "Ring for about that too. And, you probably don't believe me, but it was more than that."

"Like what?" Zhang wanting to hear it.

"You live in the shadows long enough, you get to know." The trembling had eased; maybe it was the tiny drinks, Valentina saying, "Yeah, I set it up, but not smart enough to get something up front."

"And you let his buddy into the play."

"Like I said, as dumb as them, right?"

"Unless you square it up."

Now she was looking hopeful.

"You make the call and put us together."

"They won't like that."

"Let me worry about that."

"But if I do . . ." Valentina looked like she was seeing a way out.

Putting up his finger, he stopped her, saying, "We're getting along, and maybe . . . maybe you walk away."

"With my share."

He smiled, then said, "Maybe I let you keep what Park won."

"That's about fifty grand light." She sighed, seeing there was no point in arguing. "But this time I want something up front."

He couldn't believe it. "You took the wrong people's money, you understand that?"

"I don't mean out of your own pocket, but how about an expense account, you have something like that?"

"In my line, we don't do expense accounts."

"So I just take your word?"

He got closer, the back of his hand brushing her throat, feeling the smooth skin. "You tell Angel you got another player, makes the first one look like the janitor. Tell him I just flew in, a guy tipping with hundreds. Think you can sell it?"

"If he thinks he'll get me upstairs, I can sell anything."

Zhang had no doubt of that, pointing at her phone, saying, "Make it the call of your life."

She looked like she was going to press him about the up-front money, then thought better of it, and said, "Been getting his voicemail all day long. Sick of hearing him go, 'Can't take the call, but at the beep, you know what to do . . .'"

He told her to try anyway.

So she walked back and forth a bit, rehearsed the play and punched in the number. Frowned when it rang a couple of times, thinking she'd have to leave another message, then hearing him pick up.

"Leaving all this shit on my phone, saying I owe you. I thought you were a pro." The guy sounding pissed off.

"Says the guy running off with my cash."

"I got it right here, baby, just waiting for things to settle."

"Uh huh."

"I was going to call you, you know that. What do you take me for?"

"After you went running out, I hung around, making like I was helping the guy, a victim myself. Helped him get to emergency. Later, I'm in the lobby —"

"Any cops?"

"He can't call them, you know that. Anyway, I see this other player come in, checks into the presidential suite. Guy's got a wristwatch worth more than your car. Snaps his fingers, gets people to do what he wants, tips with fifties."

"Another Asian dude?"

"Yeah, and I brushed up to him at the tables, you know, and find out he left the little woman at home, and he's here for the time of his life. About fifty Gs in chips stacked up in front of him like that big wall they got."

"Great Wall."

"Yeah, that one. Bet anything he's good for quarter of a mill easy, plus what he had on the table."

"Yeah, well, I don't know, think I'm done with it. Best we let things chill."

"The first guy got stitched up and went home. Told them at intake he fell down the stairs. I was there at emergency. The man never suspected me."

"Sure there's no cops?"

"What'd I say?"

"Okay, well, maybe I'm listening."

"So this new guy, I watched him drop like twenty Gs on one hand. Didn't even blink. Believe me, if I had time to find somebody else, we wouldn't be talking." Waiting a moment, then saying, "Plus, I thought we . . . well, never mind that now." Rolling her eyes to Zhang.

"What?"

"Forget it — just thought you and me had something, but . . ."

"Hey now, if this's some kind of game . . .'cause if it is, it's not going to end so good. You understand?"

"Says the jerk who ran out with my money."

"I told you I'd call, soon as things quieted. Planned to hand it right to you, maybe over dinner, candles and wine, all that. You and me celebrating the win."

"Okay, that sounds better." Valentina rolling her eyes to Zhang.

"So the guy we did went home, huh?"

"Told the intake nurse he took a tumble, too much CC. Got his head stitched and got on the first plane home. Put him in the cab myself. Nothing he could say about money he wasn't allowed to have in the first place."

"Okay, so uh, this new guy . . . give me a time."

"How about now? But, Angel?"

"Yeah."

"This time it's just you and me."

Dead air for a moment, then he said, "So where's your place?"

"Uh uhn. Wait in the bar, same as before."

"Why not your place?"

"Maybe when I see the money." She looked at Zhang, the man nodding.

Angel saying, "But I tell you, if I even smell a cop, or a set-up, I'm splitting, and then I'll come back and —"

She ended the call.

. . . seen better days

Fitch parked the Brave on Third, below the mall. Taking his walking stick, he didn't bother locking the RV, no point with the busted window, and he walked across the lot, going to the east entrance. A couple of homeless guys sitting outside the exit counting a cart of empties, one of them bitching about the restriction on returns, just twenty-four items a day, wanting to go to the return depot a couple of blocks away. The other one arguing, wanting a drink now.

Going past the plastic palms of the Bamboo, Fitch caught a whiff of lemongrass and ginger. The smell of food had him thinking of the meatloaf he'd missed out on. Not sure if he'd go back, guessing Dell or the cook likely called the cops. He waved to the woman behind the lotto kiosk, with its promise of scratch-and-win. Walked to the Pharmalife, checking the aisle of across-the-counter painkillers, some with ibuprofen, some with acetaminophen. Wanting something for the ghost of pain low in his belly. The cancer letting him know it was tapping at his soul, something Russell warned would worsen as the disease progressed. The ghost likely to become a hot knife poking at his chest.

Taking a box of Motrin, he went to the rack of non-script reading glasses, tried a 2.5, went to a 3.0. Reading the fine print on the side of the box, wanting to avoid anything with codeine. Putting the glasses back, he stood in line and paid the pharmacist, Fitch wondering what the hell happened to provincial health care. Used to cover stuff like this.

He'd been hanging with Milton too long, the bleak outlook was rubbing off, his friend a lifetime cynic, mistrusting all political figures, lawyers, members of the media, just about anybody in a tie, and certainly anyone in a white coat with a med degree on the wall. In Milton's mind, Bentleys and country homes were courtesy of an aging public.

A janitor pushed a cart of cleaning supplies, a push broom turned upside down like a sign of surrender. A guy near his own age, *Tony* embroidered in script on his pocket. Glancing at Fitch, he nodded a hello. Fitch nodded back, telling himself, "There's a guy, got it worse than I do." A voice inside saying, "Yeah, but has he got cancer?"

Turning into the Walmart, Fitch smiled at the greeter by the door, passed aisles of produce, cleaning products and bottled water, turning down the cereal aisle, his hip and feet aching from yesterday's fight. Yeah, but you should see the other guys. Fitch feeling good about stepping in and locking antlers, something that made him feel alive. Swinging his crutch and spraying the can, then plowing into their ride and rescuing the kid. Playing the cop one more time, twenty years since he retired. Doing what needed doing, only a little slower these days — luck and the element of surprise saving his butt. Caught himself smiling, then wondering if the two clowns were out looking for him. Not the type to let it pass.

Checking the boxes, finding what he wanted, he went past the soulless self-checkouts and lined up for the cashier — not taking work from his fellow man. Leaning on his stick, he waited behind a woman with an overflowing cart, the woman eyeing a display of after-Halloween candies, getting in some impulse-buying, tossing a couple of bags on her pile. She saw he only had a couple items and let him go ahead, Fitch thanking her.

Going out the automatic doors, he shuffled back across the lot. The autumn heat rising off the pavement felt good, and his whole body was aching by the time he got to the Brave parked in the shade of a line of poplars.

Climbing behind the wheel, he was sure it was the right thing to do: take Wren along to Peachland. Not sure what would come past that, but he wouldn't just leave her on her own. And no way he'd turn her over and let the system sort it out. No idea what she was running from, thinking she already confided about her mom dying, so that was a start. The rest would come.

And he had a good idea how Carolyn would feel about him showing up with a runaway, her with a baby on the way. But she'd come around and see he had no choice, then see past any walls the kid was sure to put up. As a matter of fact, he bet the two of them would hit it off — eventually.

Driving to Harbourside and along the vacant field, he backed the Brave into a spot, pulling tight to the curb. Taking his cell, he called up Milton, getting Minkie, and asking how the three of them were faring, hearing Wren giggle in the background, guessing Milton was telling her some tall tale. Minkie said Milton had gone off drinking beer and left her with the girl. "But to tell the truth, Fitch, the kid's an absolute delight." Then calling out and getting Milton on the line.

"How you faring, Milt?"

"Nothing's fair around here, Fitch," Milton said, making a show of it. "This kid you saddled me with . . . my God, she's skinning me at checkers. And got something she calls a damned swear jar. You know about this?"

"It's only been an hour, Milt," Fitch said.

"Cruel minutes, every one of them. I considered you a friend, Fitch. Don't know why you'd do me like this. Here I am going broke in my own place. Good God, when are you coming for her?"

Fitch hearing Milton step out of his rig, moving away from it.

"Sounds like I got back in the nick of time." Fitch set out the cereal boxes on the fold-down table: Cap'n Crunch, Cocoa Puffs, and Trix.

"One more thing," Milton said, lowering his voice. Fitch looking through the windshield, seeing him across the field.

"One of those guys came looking."

"When?"

"Twenty minutes or so." Milton telling him the rest.

When he clicked off, Fitch getting past a new stab in his chest, sharper than any so far, that one taking his wind away. Getting the Motrin bottle, remembering what it said on the label — maximum six a day. Pouring water in a glass, he popped off the lid, guessing that stab deserved three, hoping they wouldn't make him dopey. Knowing he was going to need his wits.

. . . the pain of pleasure

Nikki swung open the hotel room door and stood barefoot in the tight dress, her arm against the frame, blocking Angel from coming in, giving him attitude, something he'd expect. If the arm didn't keep him back, maybe the cold-front demeanor would. A cold front with a jigger of sex mixed in. Nikki knowing how to pour it. And she wasn't feeling bad about what was coming, this son of a bitch deserving it.

The room behind her was dark, the same room where he knocked out Park Won-Soon. Nikki counting on it all happening too fast, and this guy being too dumb and too fired up seeing her now to remember room numbers.

On the phone, she'd told Angel to meet her in the same bar while she worked up the new player. Then she called him on his cell a half hour later, told him to come upstairs, gave him this room number and hung up, now standing there and looking serious about getting paid up front.

"I got it right here, babe, like I said." Tapping his pocket. "So how about it, you gonna invite me in, we hit the mini-bar, or maybe you want to count it in the hall?"

She held out her hand, saying, "Yeah, I want to count it."

Acting like he couldn't believe it, he shoved past her and stepped in, taking charge of the situation, saying these rooms all looked alike.

"Yeah, so does money, but I still want to see it." Catching his elbow, she spun him around as she let the door shut behind her. The room near dark, except for some light spilling from the bathroom, its door half-closed.

He caught her wrist. "It's like that, huh?" Reaching in a pocket, he pulled a roll of bills, held by an elastic, showing it to her, but not handing it over. He turned in the dark, saying, "This place got a light?" Going for a wall switch, he was in far enough, seeing the shape of the man sitting on the bed. The little light coming from the bathroom showed the nickel of the pistol next to him, a suppressor on the end.

"Hey, now, what's this?"

Nikki stepped against the far wall, out of the line. Watching how both men handled it.

Zhang sat on the unmade bed, his jacket off, his white shirt with the sleeves rolled up, the collar unbuttoned, suit jacket neatly folded next to him. Enough light to show he was bigger than the player they had mugged.

"How about switching on a light here, baby?" Angel said, standing trapped. "Seems we got company."

Nikki didn't make a move.

Eyes adjusting to the dim light, Angel said, "So I come by to see my lady Valentina, pay her a visit, along with what I owe . . . So, hey, somebody want to tell me what we're playing at?" Too far from the door to jump back out.

Nikki watched Angel standing flat-footed. Zhang just looking at him from the bed, not moving, the pistol in easy reach.

"Guess I should'a seen it coming," Angel said, throwing his hands up. "You set me up, huh, baby?" Glanced her way, then back to Zhang, saying to him, "So if you're packing a badge, my friend, I believe you got to say." He lowered his hands, waited, half turning his head to her. "How about it, baby, you work a deal, reduce your sentence and throw me under the wheels? That it?"

Nobody else speaking.

"That, or he's your pimp, or it's a Murphy thing, you two working a fast one. Want it all for yourself now, that it?"

"You know, Angel, you open your mouth, you just prove my point," she said.

"What point's that?"

"You don't have all the dots on your dice."

The guy on the bed didn't show a badge, and hadn't moved, and the silencer on the end of his pistol sure wasn't cop issue.

"Your buddy here wants to make me sweat, huh?" Tilting his head, Angel looked around like he was appraising the place.

She kept her back to the wall. Zhang just sat on the bed they'd been rolling on for the past hour. Best sex she had with a man in a long time, doing it twice with plenty left in the tank.

"Okay, so you know who I am, how about you say who the hell you are?" Angel kept his hands in view. Got nothing from the guy, tipping his head back to her. "You got your friend here a little tongue-tied."

"Ought to learn when to shut up," she said to him. "Maybe do you some good."

"Be nice if somebody just told me why the fuck, who the fuck and what the fuck." Angel lowered his hands slowly, but still held them out to the sides.

Zhang just sat there, his pistol next to him.

"The money, it's about the money, that it?" Angel turned to her again, his right hand near his pocket now. "Tell me I'm getting warm, baby?"

Nikki stayed by the wall. Even in the dim light, she could see Angel was sweating, his forehead shining.

He turned his back to the guy on the bed, but still talking to her, touching his pocket now, saying, "Got your end right here, like I said I would. Just want to know who I'm handing it to, you or him?" His fingers going in the pocket, then turning back to her.

Then back to the guy on the bed, now holding the pistol and aimed at Angel's chest.

Nikki held out her hand and stopped Angel's hand from coming from the pocket, then she reached his other pocket and took out some folded bills. Counted them and said, "This is like a grand. Where's the rest?"

Angel shrugged.

Turning to Zhang, she stepped out of the way and said, "You may as well shoot him."

"Hey, hey, whoa, girl. I got it in safekeeping, every penny. Don't you worry." Angel looking from her to him, saying, "Women, huh?"

"Where is it?" Zhang said, sounding tired.

"Well, now . . ." Angel smiled, taking a breath and looking like they were getting somewhere.

"It's in your car, right?" Nikki said. "Lemme guess, the trunk? No way you'd leave it with your dumb buddy." Looking to Zhang, saying, "Guy who fell from the dum-dum tree and hit every branch going down."

Angel stared at her.

"Write the address," Zhang said, the pistol steady on him.

"Well, now, there we go, got a little dialogue happening. Address you want, huh? Maybe I can help you out."

"Bet if you take his phone, his buddy's on the speed dial," Nikki said to Zhang.

Angel turned and looked at her, couldn't believe it.

"Do it." Zhang nodded.

"Let's see it." Nikki holding out her hand.

Scowling, Angel started to reach.

"Let her get it," Zhang said.

And Angel put his hands up and took a step toward her, putting an armchair between him and the guy on the bed. Indicating his left pocket.

Reaching around him, leaning against him, she felt the pistol, took the phone, then took his hand and tapped his fingerprint, then was checking the directory and smiling. "Right there on the speed dial."

"Make the call," Zhang told her.

Nikki frowned, saying, "To the creep who asked for an employee discount?"

"Tell him his buddy's gone for a smoke, and you don't trust him. Say you want him here." Zhang wagged the pistol at her. "And Valentina, make it the call of your life."

She put on a hurt look. This guy she'd just been in bed with, taken him around the world, now getting treated like he didn't trust her.

With the armchair in front, Angel stood at an angle away from the man, slipping his hand back in the pocket, touching the Springfield, saying, "Save you some time, friend, my share's in the trunk of my 'Stang. You know what that is, a 'Stang? Half of what we took. How about I let you keep it, and I just walk out of here. How's that sound to you?"

Getting nothing.

Nikki took a step, almost between them now, saying to Zhang, "So I do this, let's be clear, what's my end?" She held the phone, giving Angel his chance.

"Maybe you get to walk," Zhang said.

Clicking the phone, still in front of Angel, she tapped the speed dial number. Sucking air, getting herself psyched, she listened to the tone, stepping by Angel.

Picking up on the third ring, Cooder said, "'S'matter, forget your little raincoats?"

"It's Valentina."

And got silence.

"Remember me, the girl you ripped off?" Nikki sounding friendly. Waiting, she said, "Jesus, say something. I can hear you breathing."

"Where the fuck's Angel?"

She heard him crunching something, the man eating on the phone. She said, "Question is, where's my money?"

"Talk to him. And why you calling on his phone?"

"What he handed me was light, about fifty-two grand. Comes here acting all take-it-or-leave-it." Her eyes on Angel's as she spoke. "And I said no way, and the asshole goes for a smoke and left his phone. So I'm calling you, thinking maybe I been talking to the wrong guy?"

"Uh huh."

"Remember you asked about an employee discount?"

"Now you're messing with me," Cooder said.

"How about I give you a taste, no charge?"

Could hear Cooder breathing on the line. Gave him a few seconds, then she said, "Tried to tell your buddy, another player's come to town, been getting acquainted. The guy's loaded and ripe for picking."

"Tell Angel to call when he comes in." And Cooder was gone.

She looked at the phone in her hand, then looked to Zhang.

"You didn't sell it," Zhang said, shaking his head. Then he told her to get the notepad by the phone, looked to Angel and said, "What's the address?"

Angel looked like he was considering, Nikki watching his hand at the pocket. He said, "So we're clear here, friend, I give up my good buddy, then what, I just walk away?"

"Car keys," Zhang said to him.

Angel smiled, his hand going in the pocket.

"Not you." Zhang nicked his head at Nikki. "You."

She hesitated, then moved off the wall and reached into Angel's pocket. And Angel grabbed her and swept her in front with his left hand, bringing the pistol out with his right.

Zhang's pistol making *pop pop* sounds.

Angel staggered and fell straight back, bounced off the wall, and ended lying in the vestibule, a gasp coming from his mouth. Zhang stood and popped him in the chest.

Nikki fell against the wall, clapping a hand over her mouth, wanting to scream but she couldn't. A dot on Angel's forehead, two more on his chest, looked like dark ink blotting his shirt, then seeping down his side and into the carpet.

Zhang turned and laid the pistol back on the bed. "Another drink?" Stepping by her, he went to the mini-bar, saying what they had left, burgundy or the bubbly. Her choice. Then asking her to switch on the light.

« « «

Handing her a glass, Zhang sipped the sparkling wine, trying to find a way around this, knowing there wasn't one, thinking it was a shame.

She downed half in a swallow like it was oxygen, her hand shaking so much the bubbly sloshed from the glass. Couldn't look at the lifeless eyes of the man on the floor.

"You two have a thing?"

"You asking if we did it?"

"Just curious."

"Never got to it . . . owing me fifty-three thousand, plus you shooting him."

"You're something, all looks on the outside, all business on the inside."

She looked at the pistol on the bed, considering her chances.

Pouring the rest of the bubbly between the two glasses. "Don't worry your head about it," he said, holding his up, then clinking her shaking glass.

She gulped hers down and watched him sit on the bed.

"Valentina, that your real name?"

"It's Nikki." In spite of the champagne, her throat was dry. Never been so scared.

"Nikki, yeah, I like it." And he picked up the pistol.

. . . *another thing coming*

Yeah, they'd jacked a string of high-end cars and made decent money. But working with Angel was getting too much. They'd met at the Black Dog in Lynn Valley all those months ago and got to talking over happy-hour nachos and a jug of Red Truck. The Canucks were a disgrace on the widescreen that night. Couldn't defend worth a shit, or win a face-off or any key battles around the net, fucking up every scoring chance. The whole line was punished and trapped on the ice. And that rookie kid they'd drafted was proving to be a shit enforcer, far from the likes of the Tiger or Gino or Brashear, something Cooder knew a thing or two about.

Both men talking about what they did for work, Cooder explaining now that he was done with hockey, he was getting his ticket, going to be fixing leaks and installing toilets. Didn't say it was the only job he could get after prison. Angel said he was in entertainment, booking acts for the hottest Gastown clubs, calling it show biz. They downed a couple more jugs after the game, and a half hour before closing time, Angel said, "Hey, how about we cut the bullshit?" Looking at Cooder, saying, "You really a plumber?"

"Yeah, well, I lay pipe." Cooder grinned, half in the bag. The safari hat crooked on his head.

"Yeah, what do you do about a slow drip?" Angel knocked the table, laughing so hard, spilling some beer.

"Drano."

"Your pipe starts dripping, Drano's the least of your worries."

Laughing, Cooder took the jug, poured the last of it in his glass, the beer long gone flat. Saying, "Okay, let's just say I'm a plumber like you're an actor."

"I said I book acts, there's a difference."

"Yeah, so who you booked?"

Angel looked at him and couldn't come up with a name.

"That's what I thought," Cooder said.

Angel ordered up another jug and was told they missed last call. Angel bitching he didn't hear nothing like a bell. The bartender telling them to get lost. The two filing out of the place, going out to the parking lot, Angel staggering to his Mustang II Ghia.

Cooder stood in front of the grill, taking a leak, facing away from the streetlights.

"Got to do that right by my ride?"

"Your ride?" Cooder finished and tucked himself in. Looking at the car, saying, "You mean the wife's car?"

"Panty catcher like this, man, means I don't need a ball-and-chain at home."

"You know it's yellow, right?"

"It's vintage cream. But don't let the looks fool you. She's got the 302 under the hood, the Edelbrock manifold, forged pistons, aluminum heads, the works." Angel tapped a hand on the hood.

"You get flagged down, somebody needs a cab?"

"Yeah, what do you drive?" Angel looked around at the near-empty lot.

"I'm out having a few pops, I flag one of you boys down, get you pulling on your meter. That or I help myself to something with an open door."

"Like steal a ride?"

"Why not?"

"How about if it's locked?"

"Then I get a coat hanger, pop it, get in and do a little rewiring."

"Been a while, huh?" Angel said. "Coat hangers and hot-wiring, man, that went out with white walls."

"Being in show business, I guess you'd know something about it."

"My slim-jim days are behind me, man. Nowadays with the new linkage, first thing you'll get is the alarm and head-lights blinking. But it doesn't mean it can't be done."

"Yeah, how do you do it?"

"Funny you should ask." Angel putting on a grin.

"I got a feeling you're gonna tell me something."

"Telling you because maybe I'm looking for the right guy."

Cooder leaned against the car, feeling the beer, but curious. "We still on stealing cars? 'Cause I'm not light in the loafers, nothing like that."

"Fuck'd make you even think that?" Angel looking repulsed.

Cooder pointed to the yellow car, like there's your answer.

"So maybe I jack cars, the entertainment's the front."

"Yeah, so?"

"That's it."

"So like, you need a lookout while you smack out a window, help yourself to an Alpine player, the Oakleys off the dash, something like that?"

"You're close, but on the wrong end of the scale, brother. That's thinking small-time."

Cooder seeing he was serious. "I'm not looking to getting locked up again."

"Yeah, suppose what you got's better, plunging toilets and laying your pipe?"

Cooder just looked at him.

"Yeah, that's what I thought."

« « «

From the jump, Angel had been after a wheelman. Fancy yellow Mustang with the V8, and the man couldn't drive for shit. His vision was fucked, had trouble judging distance since he'd been a kid. Had a fancy name for it, but it was lazy eye. Told Cooder he got into the tae kwon do to help his peripheral, earning his black belt with the stripes. The next time they met, they sat sober in Angel's living room, nice two-bedroom condo he rented in Pemberton, and he laid out how to steal cars and prosper, did it like a presentation, then said, "So, what you think?"

"Think popping a window, doing a snatch-and-grab beats it. Maybe it's not big-time, but it ain't a felony either."

"You keep thinking your nickel-and-nail shit, brother, you just limit your potential."

"Limit my potential, huh?"

"That's right. Driving through life with your brakes on. Talking about what you used to be. I'm saying, why settle for scraps when you can go whole hog? Go from the minors to the big league. Pedal to the metal and cruise down easy-money street."

"Fuck's that even mean, nickel and nail."

"A line from an old song, but forget about that. Maybe I'm just talking over your head."

"You're five six, seven, tops. Can't even see over my head. And top it off, your eyesight's the shits. Told me that yourself."

"No offense, brother, I'm not the one with trouble seeing." Angel was planting the seeds. Saying he was giving Cooder a chance to catch up and see the wreckage of his own life. "Sure you played in the minors, racked up all that penalty time, but then you took it personal, took the fight off the ice and ended up doing two years in Kent. How am I doing?" Angel had looked him up on the internet. Sure enough, the man had played in the minors. Angel talking to him now like he was dangling future salvation. Borrowing lines from a Tony Robbins CD.

Cooder wished he hadn't told him about doing time for taking a couple of hockey fights off the ice, putting one guy in a coma. Still, it was hard to argue with what the man was saying. He hated the plumbing work, apprenticing meant crawling into the dirtiest places, unclogging pipes and toilets — the foulest stink on earth. And after the last shift — showing up hungover and unable to get a spinning bolt off some lady's basement throne, he ended up losing his cool, smashing at the bolt with his channel locks — now he might not even have a job. "So, what if I say I'm in?"

"Then we go to work."

Cooder thought what the hell, asked about Angel's front, being told once in a while he booked an act, something that looked good on his tax return. And Angel taught him the ABCs about zoning in the hot spots along South Granville, Shaughnessy and Kits, Robson and Park Royal. Taught him to be on the watch for late-model imports worth over a hundred big ones. Explained about signal relaying. Took him out to what he called the workplace and told him to watch and learn.

First time was out front of the Hycroft, middle of the day, a good-looking woman, north of forty with a facelift making her believe she was south of thirty, stepped from a Bentley, a Continental GT in glacier white. Hands in his jacket pockets, Angel stepped easy along the curb in his washed denim and three-hundred-dollar tennis shoes, Versace T under the leather jacket. Tipping up his shades, saying, "You having yourself a fine day, miss?"

Her eyes like stones, the woman said she wanted her car parked, taking him for the valet. Not the type to be kept waiting.

Hand in his jacket pocket with the transmitter. Angel pushed up the smile, saying, "I look like that to you, the valet?"

"That or a toy boy. Either way ..." Pressing her key fob, she flicked the door locks, dropped the keys in her bag, her painted mouth frowning, and she walked up the steps and into the door. Did it without a doorman, en route to giving somebody shit about the AWOL valet. Angel hearing her heels clanking on the marble inside, acting like she owned the place.

The transmitter in his pocket had blocked the fob's signal. Getting in the driver's side, he pressed a second button, and the transmitter fooled the engine to life. Waving to the returning valet, he rolled down the driveway, stopped off the grounds and got out, going around the passenger side, showing Cooder how it was done.

Cooder got behind the wheel, looked at the interior, couldn't believe this ride. Holding up his hand, the two of them slapping high-fives, and Cooder drove off in the nicest ride of his life.

"Beats taping up the window and thumping out the glass, huh?" Angel said. "Easiest five bills you ever seen in your life."

Driving the nice wheels a block past the Auto Mall in North Van, tucking into a laneway, a car ring working out of a body shop, the place where Angel had been doing business. Dropping cars destined for shipping containers at the port, most of them heading overseas, a few knocked down for parts. Cooder never went in, was told to wait at a coffee bar nearby, Angel taking it from there, driving the stolen cars around back of the garage and getting their money. Walking to the café, handing Cooder five hundred, what he said was half.

Worked it the same way every time, Angel locating a car, Cooder nearby with the transmitter. Angel acting nonchalant as the driver parked it, nodding at Cooder — yeah, this one. Cooder working the buttons, and the two of them getting in and driving off. Played it the same way every time and nobody suspecting a thing. Lexus, Jag, Benz and Beemer all in the first week. Cooder up five hundred a pop with no income to declare.

Angel kept the connection to himself, calling it a need-to-know thing, telling Cooder the boys in the shop were funny about bringing new people on board. Angel explaining it was for his own good, insulating Cooder in case of some cop investigation went down. Cooder waiting a block away at the Grind coffee bar while Angel took in the hot wheels. Came back and handed him his cut. Didn't matter about the make or model. All paid the same, five hundred bucks. All Cooder had to do was work the transmitter, block the owner's signal, then do the driving. Grand theft auto with low risk and a sweet return. Sure beat plumbing or punching it up on the ice.

Angel always coming back from the body shop with that cock-eyed grin, sometimes with a "shopping list." Benzes, Beemers, Caddies and Lincolns topping the list, followed by Infiniti Gs and Audis. Other times they just went out and scored what ever they could find, as long as it was high-end. The best time was when they rolled from Shaughnessy Golf and Country in an NSX Acura in "curva" red. Practically had to lie down to get in the two-seater, Cooder putting the pedal down and going "*Woo-hoo*," feeling the g-force, zero to sixty in under three seconds. Even better than scoring the Bentley. Thought he'd died and gone to heaven, resisting the urge to punch it and fly across the Lions Gate, Angel playing nanny and saying they couldn't risk it. Man, he would've jacked that ride for free.

Angel let Cooder crash on the Ikea mattress in the guest room of his top-floor suite, took two hundred bills off him every week to cover rent, plus another hundred for groceries. Cooder paying for his own beer and snacks. Angel starting to leave hints about him getting his own digs, feeling it was for the best. Two dozen cars that first month and Cooder was feeling flush, and starting to feel his partner's cold shoulder of resentment. Angel bitching about him leaving towels on the floor, eating all the Ben & Jerry's, crumbs next to the toaster, complaining about stains from the Cheetos. Saying how would it look if he had a lady friend spend the night. Truth be told, Cooder was getting tired of Angel's company too, his constant bullshit. He'd gotten to the point where it was high time to get his own place.

Finally when he went to see Valentina, Angel told him to respect the fine Italian leather he was sitting his ass on, Cooder splayed in front of Angel's widescreen, a bowl of Cheetos on his lap and his feet on the glass coffee table.

Angel bitching, "You're getting that orange shit everywhere, brother." Pointing to a fresh streak on his fine leather. Cooder telling him it washed off.

"Yeah, well, next time I dial in Molly Maid, it's coming out of your end, brother." Then Angel was heading to the

Rock, looking forward to seeing her, acting like he was on a date, sporting his Brooks Brothers pinstripes, an electric-blue tie looped in a Windsor. The man spritzing on what he called his signature scent. Just not a natural smell on a man. And leaving that spoor in the jacked cars too — his signature scent like evidence.

Leaving Cooder to his American Idols, Angel slipped on his shades, covering the lazy eye, stepped out and got in his taxi-yellow 'Stang, and drove off. Cooder wondering how all of a sudden the man could drive. Truth of it, Cooder was happy for the alone-time, fed up listening to Angel running his mouth while he played chauffeur, all for five bills a pop.

And it had been the same thing week in, week out. And this had been a busy seven days, starting with the Panamera out front of the Trump, the owner leaving the four-ways flashing and going inside. Next up an M-Class from the Public Market lot at Granville Island, a week's worth of groceries in the hatch, then a C-Class fresh off the dealer lot in North Van, a retired schoolteacher taking a test drive, inside the dealership getting hustled by the salesman. Cooder working the transmitter and the two of them driving off. Waiting at the same coffee shop every day, having a flat white or an affogato. Cooder on a first-name basis with Lucia the barista, all that caffeine buzzing through him like electrical current. Cooder sitting there thinking he wouldn't mind giving Lucia a jump, the woman starting to look alright to him since the trouble with Tracy.

He'd been keeping his cash in the bottom of his hockey bag, under his laundry — counted it every day, make sure he wasn't light — didn't trust his partner, but he couldn't put it into a Vancity account with no way to explain it after he told the owner of Roland's Plumbing what he could do with his shit job.

It was a repeat of the show he missed the night before, the Idols were down to five now, and Cooder was trying to get his mind off business, getting caught up in the show for the second time around, chomping Cheetos and rooting for Tiffany, this black chick with a voice that could shatter glass, a nice rack too, an easy win if Simon Cowell got his head out of his ass long enough to make the obvious choice. Now there was a guy — man, he'd love to swipe that fucker's personal ride, teach him a lesson about being human. And what was with that T-shirt, two sizes too small, belonging on some underaged kid with acne.

Then his cell rang and he thought it might be Tracy again, asking how come he didn't come around. He glanced at the display, seeing the call was from Angel.

... *thinking it through*

I t felt wrong to Cooder from the start. Angel got all
dressed up and had gone to see this Valentina again.
The two of them had walked out of the Rock with all the
money, agreed they would teach the bitch a lesson about
getting greedy. Since the score, she'd been leaving messages
on Angel's cell, one after another, telling him how pissed she
was, wanting her cut. Finally telling him she had something
better, wanted to see him alone, lay it out for him. Angel
saying to Cooder it couldn't hurt to find out. Cooder saying
he was just thinking with his dick, going to see her, putting
on his bullshit moves, expecting to get her legs scissored
around his back, slipping in the greasy monkey. Angel with
his cock-eyed, shit-eating grin.

Sitting on the couch, eating his way to the bottom of the
bag of Cheetos, Cooder swiped his fingers on the leather
cushion, getting rid of the salt and crumbs. He pictured it,
Angel coming back, bragging how he rode this chick to glory.
Hearing her out about an even bigger score, another loaded
Asian coming to town.

After the Idols, this Valentina called from Angel's phone, telling Cooder Angel shorted her — no surprise there — and the chick knew how much they scored, Cooder guessing Angel completely lost his mind, telling her that. Saying she didn't trust him, how she wanted Cooder sitting in on this deal.

It felt wrong, and he hung up, expecting Angel to call back. Sitting there staring at the phone that didn't ring again, Cooder started thinking Angel and the chick were setting him up, a double-cross. The two of them coming after his share. Fifty-three grand being enough for Angel to sell out his own mother. And Angel knew where Cooder kept his money stashed.

Crunching up the bag, he tossed it on the coffee table, put the hockey bag by the door. Grabbing his toothbrush and razor, his extra chinos, shirts, jockeys, socks and jacket. Taking one of Angel's pillowcases, part of a matching set. Three hundred thread-count. Putting his stuff in it. Set it next to the hockey bag by the door, then got Angel's car-swiping transmitter from behind the TV.

Sliding his jaw side to side, still sore from the Asian guy getting in that lucky shot. The guy scraping his shoe down Cooder's shinbone and stomping his instep. Yelling, "Ha." The front of his leg had already gone eggplant. Wouldn't mind strangling the little fuck with his own black belt, but that score had been settled in Cooder's mind, Cooder up over fifty grand for his pain and troubles. He knew he had to get clear of Angel and the chick. It was the old man in the kamikaze camper, that still begged for some closure.

His cell toned again, and Cooder looked at Angel's name on the display, thinking he took his sweet time calling him back, going to hand him some bullshit about getting delayed on the Lions Gate, taking a little longer to get there. Who knew, maybe he did get lucky, and he had his head turned around by pussy. Cooder could see him walk in with that wet grin, raising his Springfield and blasting away. Taking all the money and splitting it with the chick.

Cooder considered his play. One way: take off now. The other way: tuck behind the door and clothesline the son of a bitch coming in, say, "Surprise, motherfucker." Put him on his ass, tell him he quit. And if the chick was there, ask her, "You need a lift someplace, baby? Maybe put in some time with a real man." Do to Angel what he surely had in mind for him. Cooder betting Angel's share was in the trunk of his taxi-yellow ride, which would be parked out front when Cooder left him leaking blood and spitting teeth. And he'd drive away with all the money, wouldn't even feel bad about it.

The phone chirped again, and Cooder glanced at it. It was Tracy's name on the display. He wasn't getting into it, not again. He was done with her and that bun in the oven.

It was time to blow. He'd square things with Angel, leaving the only regret — not catching up with the old geezer first.

He sat on the arm of Angel's couch, adding the sum of Angel's share to his own — all the money he'd ever need. Then he thought maybe the Canucks bag had been empty when Angel left. Just made it look like he had it with him, not wanting Cooder to get any ideas — the kind he was having now.

He went to Angel's bedroom closet, hesitating, thinking the doorknob could be booby-trapped. Tapping a finger at the brass knob. Not rigged, but locked. Recalled Angel saying how he rigged a car battery to his back doorknob one time, repelled some degenerated speed fiends from stealing the drugs he'd been dealing to them. Wouldn't put it past his partner to rig something like that now, nobody trusting each other.

Squaring up in front of the closet door, Cooder drove his boot through it, hinges twisting, wooden teeth biting into the meat of his eggplant calf.

Fuck!

Careful pulling his leg back out, the splinters hurting like hell. He opened the door, looking at the packed closet. Feeling past the suits, pressed shirts and hanging pants, then patting along the top shelf. Nothing in there but fucking clothes. Then he pushed the piece of wood aside and felt around up in the attic space. Nothing.

So the Canucks bag was in the trunk of the Mustang. Finishing the last Bud from the fridge, Cooder ran scenarios through his mind. The chick poisoning Angel with thoughts like it was Cooder who botched the play in the hotel room, Angel having to jump in and crack the Asian with the pistol. Yeah, no doubt in Cooder's mind, Angel was lost to the power of the cooz, coming to do him dirty. Wanting it all. Take Cooder out and he and the chick would get down to some mattress pounding, doing it with Cooder bleeding out on the floor — his dead eyes watching them going at it. A fucked-up threesome, two coming, and one going.

And like that, his mind was made up, and he knew what to do.

... *the jumps*

The girl dug into the Cocoa Puffs like it was the best thing ever in a bowl. Fitch looked out the side window, still felt the two men would come looking — worried how much the girl overheard in back of the SUV, enough to put them away. And an old man with a walking stick and a colostomy bag did them like that — not something their kind could let go. Fitch smiling, thinking about it again. Feeling a jab behind his ribs, the cancer knocking.

"Sorry, am I crunching too loud?" Wren looked at him, spooning cereal.

"Music to my ears, kid. You go on, enjoy."

"My mom said I slurp sometimes. I guess when it's good, I forget, and I go too fast."

Beautiful thing about hearing aids, Fitch thought, looking out the front, you could turn them down too, and nobody's the wiser. He had a good vantage from where he was parked. And he had Milton across the field, knowing he'd be looking out.

Wren shook more cereal from the box, going to the Danby for the carton of milk, popping the spout and pouring it on top, feeling right at home.

"There's a banana, you want?"

"With Cocoa Puffs, really?" And she was back to crunching.

And he was back to thinking of Peachland, driving the old Brave, planned on leaving first thing in the morning.

. . . *Zhang bang*

You kill in wartime and they call it serving your country — doesn't matter which country, any country — and doing it with God on your side. Do it enough and they pin a medal on you and call you a hero. Zhang put in three years with special ops. Maybe at one time he bought what the People's Liberation Army was selling. Once back in private life, he'd been approached by the Bamboo Union, hired on as a contractor to the triad, paying him more for all that talent and training than he could turn down.

Bending, he fished the keys from Angel's pocket and stepped over the bodies. Shame about the woman, couldn't get himself to look at her now. As much as he had used her, she had reeled him in, the woman smart and funny, and they'd been getting along. Saying her real name at the end. Nikki. Zhang thinking they could have carried on their thing. And it would have been good — for a while, anyway.

She'd been cool even when he raised the pistol, looking at him. Maybe she didn't believe he'd do it. Promising to keep her mouth shut, then giving him that smile, looking him in the eyes, and saying but that wouldn't be any fun.

He saw her hand going in her bag, guessing why, And he shot her. Just a pop. There was a moment of disbelief in her eyes, and he watched her fall, pointing the pistol to the back of her head, but seeing it was done. Looking in her handbag, seeing her piece — looking out for herself, right to the end.

He let the door lock behind him and took a rear exit. Matching the number on the old-style license-plate fob, he found the Mustang, the money in the Canucks bag inside the trunk, right in plain view. And he got in and rolled north through Richmond, going to collect the rest of the triad's money from the address on the dead man's driver's license.

Crossing the bridge at Burrard, he turned onto Pacific, swinging onto Beach, then onto Denman. Two guys coming out of the Three Brits from an afternoon of drinking stumbled into the street. The one guy slapped the hood of the Mustang, leaning to the windshield, calling, "Hey, asshole, watch the fuck out. Yeah, you." His buddy laughed, backing him up, calling, "Get your license with your cereal, box of fuck-nuts flakes." One throwing a finger, the other crotch-grabbing, both of them bumping elbows and making it over the road.

Getting to West Georgia, Zhang turned toward the park, driving through the pines, heading for the North Shore. A homeless couple walked along with a dog, a guitar case and packs on their backs and bags under their arms.

A sports car roared up from behind him, flashing high beams at him, switching into the opposing lane, accelerating and cutting sharp in front of him, the kid driving the i8 blared the horn — maybe sixteen years old — roaring off at double the speed limit. Lotusland jam-packed with assholes of all ages just begging to be killed.

« « «

Finding a spot out front, he parked and stood on the sidewalk. Zhang Lee looked up and down the street. Nothing but a line of parked cars, somebody in their yard, trimming a yew hedge. Looking at the address, a three-story apartment building in the West Coast style, exposed timbers and board and batten, Zhang walked up the concrete steps, hit a buzzer, any buzzer, and said he was FedEx, caught the door on the buzz and went in, plastic ferns in the lobby, the funk of laundry coming from down the hall.

Ignoring the first-generation elevator, he took the back stairs up to three. Somebody cooking an early supper of onions and pork. He stood to the side of 308, waited and listened. The silenced pistol down along his side, back to his Snow Leopard days, the hard training stamped into his cells.

Fingers touched the knob, he turned it and the door opened. Wasn't locked. Counting to five, he went in low and quick, moved out of the hall's light and ended in a squat with the pistol up. Eyes darting left and right, feeling the silence. Alone.

The closet in the bedroom had been busted, looked like somebody kicked it in. Angel's partner must have caught something in Nikki's voice on the phone, figured it was wrong and fled out of there.

« « «

Leaving the building, walking along the street to the Alfa, Cooder spotted Angel's yellow car coming far up the street. Stepping behind a hedge, he set down the bag and pillowcase, seeing his chance to settle with Angel coming right to him — sure they were coming to rip him off. Except there was no woman in the car. The Mustang parked down the block, and it wasn't Angel getting out. An Asian guy stood and looked at the building, then went up the steps and looked at the intercom before going inside.

It wasn't the guy they robbed, but could be tied to him, or the money. Caught up with Angel and got his share back, along with Angel's car, and was coming for the rest of it. Cooder getting a bad feeling Angel got himself in trouble, and maybe the woman was in on it. He stood there thinking of a move. If the guy going in the building took the money off Angel, it could be in the car.

He could just run, but when had he ever run from a fight? Made his way through the minors scrapping every chance he got. Sucking in the resolve, he stepped from the hedge and went to the back of the Alfa and popped the trunk, laid his stuff in, found the S-bend lug wrench, hefted it, tucked it under his jacket and walked up the street. Standing at the overhang, putting together the game plan.

Getting his key, he let himself back in the building. Going past the elevator and up to three by the back stairs. Waiting in the stairwell, he watched through the glass of the fire door, Angel's apartment door closed. It was twenty minutes before he opened the hallway door and walked past the apartment, glanced down and saw no light from under the crack. Cooder betting the Asian was waiting in there for him.

Going down to the second floor by the front stairs, along the hall and back up the rear stairs, he stood behind the fire door again. Waiting with the lug wrench in his hand. Stood there for another half hour before a door opened farther down the hall, one of the neighbors coming from his apartment with a bag of trash, coming his way.

The door to 308 opened as the man with the trash passed, the Asian coming out, nodding to the other man. Both men coming this way, Cooder ducked back, then pulled the door open with his left hand, the lug wrench out of sight, the neighbor going through first.

Then the Asian man gave him a nod as he stepped through. Cooder saw the hand go in the pocket as he swung the iron in an arc. Hit the guy's right arm and shoved him hard, checking him into the concrete wall. Left hand grabbing the wrist.

The neighbor yelling, "What the hell's going on?" Then rushing down the stairs, getting out of the way, saying he was calling the cops.

Cooder swung the lug wrench again, the guy blocking it and knocking it away, the iron clanging onto the concrete, the man striking at Cooder's eyes, almost the same motion. Crowding him, Cooder tried to wrap him up, controlling the gun. Not letting go of the wrist. Catching a hard elbow to his chin, then a backfist to the face as he swung the smaller man around in his left arm and launched him off the stairs. Losing his grip on the gun hand.

The neighbor still yelling from somewhere below.

Pistol coming from the jacket pocket as the guy landed on his feet. Cooder rushed a couple of steps, grabbed the lug wrench and threw it, then dove at him. Sent an elbow for the head, the guy going under it, striking the back of Cooder's head, pushing him into the landing's wall. Then kicking the back of his knee, folding Cooder. Twisting, Cooder caught hold of hair and dragged the man down. Clutching the gun hand as the guy tried to point the long barrel, the silencer in the way. Catching him with a head butt, Cooder felt the nose snap, blood flowing down his face. The man didn't hesitate, struck him with his palm and snapped Cooder's head back, sent another blow to his ear. But Cooder held that wrist, crowding him, using his size.

Struck by a knee, then another elbow. The guy twisted from his grip, diving under Cooder's roundhouse swing, pulling the trigger — the popping sound — the bullet going by Cooder's cheek, tearing a chunk from the concrete. Cooder slammed the man's arm against the wall, tried knocking the pistol away. The guy spearing fingers at his eyes. Cooder kept crowding, swinging short punches. The guy blocked and countered with his left. Cooder catching a thunderclap against his ear. The world spinning, Cooder clutched hair, hanging onto the gun hand, driving the man back, slamming his skull into the wall. Taking a palm strike under the chin, jarring his teeth, then another a blow to the sternum. No linesmen jumping in to break this one up. Cooder kept holding and crowding, using his weight the way he'd learned to do on the ice, ducking his head down. Didn't matter what the guy threw. Cooder got his left arm around the guy's back, held the wrist with his right, lifted him off his feet, taking a knee to the groin for it. The guy trying to turn the pistol.

And Cooder pitched them both off the stairs, flying down the full flight — the pistol firing — Cooder controlling that wrist, twisting and landing on top. Feeling the snap of bones.

They lay in a pile. Cooder breathing hard, getting his right hand free, he smashed it into the man's face. The man was looking up, blood coming from his busted nose. The pistol was near him, but he was unable to move. The look in his eyes said he couldn't believe he'd been whipped. The hole in his chest said he'd shot himself. Blood staining his shirt and pooling down under him.

"Where the fuck's Angel?"

The guy just stared at him.

Cooder reached in the guy's jacket pocket, found a wallet. Patted his pants pockets and got the keys to the

Mustang. Hearing voices in the hall above him, more neighbors wondering what the fuck.

Taking the pistol, he left the guy lying there, no idea if he'd make it, and he limped down the stairs. In spite of all the pain, he was feeling like he won, like all those times he'd skated for the penalty box, his opponent lying behind him on the ice, the rest of the team cheering him. Cooder knowing he'd done his job.

He walked out of there and crossed the street, getting his hockey bag and the pillow case from the Alfa's trunk, putting it in the backseat of the Mustang. No time to check the trunk. He got in and drove out of there before the cops came.

He had to dump the pistol and knew the pier to toss it from. Then he'd drive east, spend a night in Kamloops, then cross the Rockies. And he'd disappear.

... *the decliners*

S topping the Mustang by the engineering firm next to the Burrard Yacht Club, first thing he did was pop the trunk. And there it was, the Canucks bag. Leaning in, he unzipped it, seeing the cash, re-zipping it and closing the trunk. He would've tossed the keys in the air, catching them one-handed, except for the pain.

Trying to hide the limp, going through the opening security gate, following an elderly couple driving their Jag, here for a social event at the clubhouse. Cooder waved like he knew them, the couple giving a weak wave back, no idea who he was.

Counting on the poor eyesight of old folks, Cooder walked on, kept his head turned from the security monitors. He walked along the dock, past a line of cruisers and harbor boats, the .38 in his pocket. Walking to the end, he glanced around, then pitched the piece into the dark waters. Going back to the car, he opened the door and started to get behind the wheel. Then he stopped.

Couldn't believe it, squinting into the lowering sun, Cooder put a flat palm up like a shield, looking west across the vacant field. And there it was, the Happy fucking Camper.

Good shit does come in threes. Putting things right with one Asian guy for the sins of another, and ending up with all the money — and now this. "Thank you, Jesus."

Didn't matter he was an old man leaning on a stick, and it didn't matter Cooder was hurt, the old man had it coming. One good shot would do it. Be like thumping his fist into head cheese, meat bits with gelatin. Whatever Cooder had left in the tank, he was knocking grandpa's dentures into next week.

Getting behind the wheel, he rolled along Harbourside, looking at the Winnebago as he went by it — the crumpled bumper and ladder, the tire with no cover. No doubt it was the right one. Curtains pulled over the tinted window on the side. Couldn't tell if the old man was inside. Another filthy camper drove from the direction of the Auto Mall, swinging wide around him, the homeless on wheels coming to squat for the night, hiding from bylaw enforcement.

Pulling onto Fell, Cooder circled the block surrounding the field, passing a woman walking a couple of setters, a half dozen Evo cars. Rolling around the corner, he pulled past an extended van and parked behind a tractor trailer, nearly across from the Happy Camper.

The harbor behind him, the dropping sun glinting off the downtown windows. Stepping to the door, he rapped, ready with, "Hey, how's your short-term memory, Pops? You remember caning me and smashing my ride?" Or could go with, "Hey, old pard, you up for the best two out of three?" Or how about, "Time's up, hero for a day's come to an end." Slam his fist into the head-cheese face, shove his way in as the old man fell back. Prop him up on the floor, and give him a couple more. Then search the place. These geezers didn't trust banks, something they carried forward from the Depression era. Maybe find the guy's life savings squirreled under a mattress, or the bottom of a coffee can.

"Help you out there, Cooder?"

Nearly jumped, but Cooder did a slow turn. Three old boys stood there — couldn't believe they got behind him like that. In their leisure wear, two in cardigans, one wearing a vest. The two flanking wearing specs.

Cooder grinned, recognizing the guy who'd been sitting on his little patch of grass, drinking Cooder's beer. "Forgot your name, old pard."

"Forgot the six-pack too." The old guy smiled.

"Guess you lied to me, that you didn't know this guy."

"You got me."

"So, what are you boys, like the security?" Cooder guessing he could blow all of them over — like puffing out birthday candles.

"You're looking at the boondock bouncers," the same old guy said, nodding at the Winnebago.

"Don't look like any of you'd bounce too good. More like busting chalk." Cooder had tossed the pistol off the dock, but it didn't matter — wouldn't need it for these guys.

The oldster to the left pushed his glasses up his nose. Gray wisps in a comb-over. The one to the right had a middle like dough. But all of them standing their ground.

"Looks like you just drift to trouble." The old guy noting the welts and bruises starting on Cooder's face.

"Yet here I am."

"How about state your business, and make it the truth this time?"

Cooder just grinned.

"Let me try another way," Milton said. "I think you should go while you can, and not come back." Nothing friendly in the way he was talking now. Blue veins showing in his drooping cheeks, craters and creases across his face. His checkered pants pulled halfway to his armpits.

"Guy owns this rig, he in there?" Cooder moved to the door. He reached for the handle. The window he'd busted covered in cardboard.

The three men closed behind him.

"Really fellas, come on now. Fun's over, huh?" Cooder said, turning to them. "Don't you got lawn bowling, shuffleboard, something like that? Really hate to knock you around."

Nobody moved.

Shaking his head, Cooder said to Milton, "You switch up your meds, old man? I'm not going to tell —"

The RV door with the cardboard over the busted-out window opened, banging into Cooder. The three old men crowding him.

Head-cheese looked out, his walking stick in hand.

Milton saying he could stay inside. "We've got this."

"Nonsense, Milt." Fitch stepped from the RV, using the walking stick to push Cooder back a step.

"Well, there we go, the geezer with the crushing camper." Cooder glared at him, his back to the others. "You owe me some money, pal."

"I don't think so."

"And what'd you do with the kid?"

"She can't hurt you."

"How about you cough up five hundred, the money I lost on that ride, maybe another five for my troubles, and we'll call it square."

"Never learned the ABCs of life, have you, son?" Fitch shook his head like he was sad about it.

"And you want to set me straight. Go from C-nile to D-mentia. Is that it?"

Two more oldsters came around the front of the Winnebago and stood watching, one of them a woman, six of them now. The new man holding a croquet mallet down along his leg. The woman holding a white sock, filled with something, probably pennies.

"I interrupting your game, fellas?" Cooder laughed, couldn't believe it, putting his hand in his pocket, standing easy. Couldn't believe five minutes ago he threw away the pistol. Then turning to the circle around him, still not seeing he'd have a problem.

Looking back at Fitch, the old man was now aiming a .22 at him, the circle of boondockers tight around him, like they were keeping Cooder from escape. The one called Milton told him to take his hand from his pocket.

Cooder grinned, looking at the pistol in the veiny hand — taking his own hand from his pocket, dangling the car keys. Saying, "You ever shoot a gun, old man?"

One of the old guys behind him snatched the keys from his fingers and tossed them down the sidewalk. Cooder half turned his head, and Fitch poked him with the barrel.

"Joined the RCMP the year they moved into the Cloverdale building. Stood at attention while they raised the flag that first time. Chief put me on the new breathalyzer van, and the first week I pulled over a car, just a routine stop, two guys got out shooting at me. First time I drew my duty weapon, put one man down, got the other one in cuffs." Fitch kept the pistol steady in his hand. His eyes stayed on Cooder's. "First time I shot it for real, not counting training."

"You get that from a movie, some old John Wayne flick? Love the Duke, huh? Yeah, me too."

"Funny thing, neither of those men had been drinking. Thought I was after them for the gas station they'd just robbed."

The circle of old men widened now, giving Fitch room to step forward and lean on the crutch. The pistol pressed into Cooder's middle.

Fitch kept talking, "Next time I fired my weapon was during a hostage situation. Bank robbery in Surrey gone wrong. We got the wheelman, but the two trapped inside wouldn't surrender, and wouldn't let the hostages go, six of them. I was part of the team going in. Both men wanting to shoot it out. Two officers went down, yours truly being one of them, taking a bullet in the thigh that time. But we kept them from doing harm to the hostages, what we set out to do."

"That how you got that?" Cooder glanced down at the crutch.

Fitch saying, "Not even close."

And Cooder grabbed, jerking Fitch's arm in the air, taking the pistol from him. Started to say, "You're long past those —"

And he was struck from behind, started to turn with the pistol, but the world kept right on turning. Old hands grabbed for it as he squeezed the trigger, trying to shoot the one with the mallet, the shot going wild into the air.

Then the crutch came up between his legs from behind, and it staggered him, that dull ache in his groin. Cooder giving a low groan as his knees went weak. Somebody taking the .22 from him.

And Fitch bent down to him and kept talking. "A time like that, you just forget everything in your world, everything that matters to you, and you do what you have to do."

Cooder started to push himself up, couldn't believe it. Wiped the side of his face with his hand, looking at blood on his fingers. "Know what they do to old dogs, huh?"

"It's all about fortitude, son. Not something I expect you to copy. Just doing what you have to to get through."

"You think I don't know about getting through?" Cooder getting his knees under him, his groin throbbing.

"Don't think you have a clue."

And Cooder jumped at him, his hands going for the throat, going to put this old dog down.

The old man moved, swinging his stick. A burst like an exploding bulb, a flash in back of Cooder's skull. And the sidewalk came up in a twisted rush. Caught in a what-the-fuck moment, he was looking at the kid, the same one who jumped out the back of the Expedition, stepping from the motor home, picking something off the sidewalk and hurrying away across the street. He could see her sneakers from under the Winnebago's chassis, thinking the kid was running away again.

Goddamn. He tried to push himself to his knees, his world spinning. Forcing himself to pull it together. The blood taste in his mouth. His fingers went to the knot at the back of his head, his vision blurred. He looked up at the old man, two faces merging into one. Cooder saying, "Kind of wood is that?"

"Hickory." The one called Fitch was bending down to him, putting his weight on the damned walking stick, wagging the .22, saying, "Fortitude and moxy, the two things I learned back then. That and a set of eyes in the back of the head. And looking at you, son, I can say you're never going to make it, not without any of that. Mark it down. It'll serve you where you're going."

The old folks around him mumbled like they knew it too. Then Cooder lay back, unable to get up, and he watched the white socks in sandals, the sensible shoes all shuffling away. He heard the Winnebago's engine catch, its tires rolling, the shadow of it rolling past him. Then the sound of more engines.

And when he could, he sat up, not ready for the flush of vomit, spewing it over the sidewalk, wishing he'd puked on those white socks and sandals. Thinking, *Who the fuck wears white socks with sandals?* The old guy had said something about needing eyes in back of his head. Second time this week he could've used them. Cooder thinking maybe he'd been hit on the head one time too many, all those years on the ice. Always getting hit. Remembering the oldster with the mallet, the old woman swinging a white sock full of pennies, making a sling out of it, doing a David and Goliath thing. Fitch with his hickory. The old fucks putting him down — doing it from behind.

When he finally pushed to his feet, his knees were jelly, not wanting to take his weight. He tried to call out to the woman walking the setters, remembering her from before. She kept on, glanced over, talking into her cell phone, hurrying the dogs away from him.

Likely heard the shot and was calling the cops. Or he was just another wino who'd had too much sauce. Not hard to believe down in this part of town.

Stupid to come here when he already had it all, looking to even a final score. Never learned that, when to quit. Should have driven out of there, just lived with the fact an old man had whipped his ass.

His head was pounding and spinning, and he felt his insides rush up. Blatting it out again. Leaning past his shoes and throwing porridge on the weeds and thistles off the sidewalk. Sitting on the rough ground, he felt a clot under his ass. Needed a minute to pull himself together, betting he had a concussion. Had enough of them back on the ice to know the feeling.

The sinking sun reflected off a barge out in the inlet, shadows stretched off the school building and trees to the west. The old folks were gone in their rigs. Feeling another wave of sick, Cooder laid back and watched dark, rolling clouds, long grass and weeds wagging in the breeze. A throbbing behind his ear. Touching a finger to the blood.

When he could get up, he was stepping onto the boulevard, and his foot shot forward, Cooder doing a Michael Jackson slide on a patch of dog shit, catching himself from going down. Cooder's head snapping from the jolt.

"The fuck's wrong with people?" Goddamn doggers, letting their mutts make the world their toilet. Then hearing distant sirens coming from Marine. And he saw it, the open driver's door of the 'Stang, the keys dangling from the lock. Cooder moved to it, looking in.

"Fuck!"

Blood pounding behind his eyes.

And he remembered seeing the kid's feet from under the camper. Fighting the spins, he retched again. Taking the keys, he hurried to the trunk, knowing it was gone.

. . . *gravy train*

Wren had heard the angry voices and drew back the curtain, looking out the side window. Fitch and Milton and the rest of the boondockers stood in a circle around the bald guy, the same one from the SUV. The one called Cooder. Bigger than any of them and half their age. Wren guessing he'd come for her. No sign of the one called Angel.

Fitch was doing the talking, leaning on his walking stick. Looked calm, almost kind, with that way of his. The big man turned to the others after somebody said something to him. And Fitch pulled a pistol in his free hand, pointing it at Cooder when he turned back. Wren couldn't believe it, her heart jumping.

Cooder pulled his car keys from his own pocket, then had them taken from behind, the keys tossed away. Then he snapped the pistol from Fitch's hand and tried to turn it on him. The pistol going off, Wren ducking down. Then coming up, worried for Fitch, seeing the croquet mallet streaking the air. Wander Woman swinging a sock, and the big man staggered. The picket of old men crowding around.

Fitch hitting him with his stick. And like that, she knew what to do.

Using the commotion, she jumped out and grabbed the keys with the Mustang fob off the sidewalk, going past the headlights, keeping the Winnebago between her and the men. Crossing to the yellow car, the one she'd seen Cooder drive up in, catching him looking from underneath the RV — the man flat on his back — not sure if he was conscious or not. She opened the door, looked on the backseat, recognizing the bag.

. . . the dust-up

Angel's bag was still in the trunk. Thanking Jesus, Cooder unzipped it and looked at half the money inside. Cooder felt the lump growing on his head, sore to the touch, remembering the game with the mallets from when he was a kid, called it wickets. Used to set the hoops in a double-diamond in the grass, about ten feet apart, the kids on the block knocking balls through the hoops, going for the last one with the peg behind it.

The last of the campers had pulled away, Wander Woman painted across on the rear of some cancered van, its exhaust loud.

The sirens were louder now. More than one. Coming past the Auto Mall, from the only way out.

No way he'd been able to drive out of here. The only chance was to run across the dog-mined field, along the Spirit Trail, past the trees where the eagles nested, and get the hell out of there. Let them yell stop all they wanted. He'd just keep running on the Spirit Trail, past the yacht club, the footbridge crossing Mosquito Creek, along a line of floating homes, past the Marine Campus and the park.

Maybe dive off the pier and swim off in the dark water. Come back for the money in the trunk later.

But that chisel strike he felt inside his skull kept him from moving. He had nothing left, none of the fucking fortitude the old man had talked about. Cooder got in and put his hands on the wheel, looking up at the heavens, saying, "What's your fuckin' problem?"

Flashing lights and sirens swept from both directions around the field.

"Police! Show me your hands."

Sitting behind the wheel of the Mustang. He sat with his hands on the wheel, and just for a moment he wanted to reach under the seat for the pistol that was gone, guessing what it would get him. Then he figured with his luck, they'd just tase him.

Cooder just sat there, feeling he'd been ejected from the game of life. Getting sent back to the penalty box at Kent. When he finally stepped from the vehicle, his hands in the air, he was wondering how the Chief was doing.

. . . *walking in cake*

"You two'll hit it off, guarantee you that." Fitch looked at Wren and smiled, took about twenty miles of driving before he convinced her he was alright. Saying he never felt better. Then telling her some more about Carolyn and what Peachland was like. Wren asking all kinds of questions, wanting to know about his daughter, the kind of music she liked, what she was into, her age, her looks.

Fitch thinking, here they were making another getaway, just left a thug lying on the sidewalk, the Brave sounding like it wasn't going to make it halfway, a shimmying and grinding sound coming again from its back end. And now Wren was asking what there was for kids to do in Peachland.

"You're gonna find out," he told her. Thinking with any luck, he'd make the rest stop in Abbotsford, and they could overnight there. At best, his retired shield would have the local mounties cutting them some slack. At worst, they'd be asked to move along. And if he couldn't drive on, they'd likely have the Brave towed, then they'd start asking questions, like who was the girl.

His cell toned, and Milton said he'd been checking the boondockers forum online, saying the Chilliwack Walmart was camper friendly, where the rest of them were heading right now.

Fitch said he'd see them there and hung up. With any luck, he'd get the Brave patched up tomorrow, and from there, he'd make it to the public land near Vedder Mountain, a place he'd camped once with Annie and Carolyn. And there were a couple more spots he knew along the Crowsnest: the hydro land by Jones Lake, the rest area at Hunter Creek, another one at Silver Lake. And if the old girl got them as far as Riverside by Keremeos, he could call Carolyn to come pick them up. Then he realized he was mumbling to himself. Looking at Wren, he smiled and winked. "You see that sign, we just passed Wynd."

She shook her head and grinned at him, said that was another quarter, then looked thoughtful, and said, "What you did back there . . ."

"Old people do that, talk to themselves."

"I mean standing up to that guy, about twice your size."

"And half my age."

"And the second time you did it."

"Because it needed doing."

She unbuckled her lapbelt and went over and hugged him.

"It wasn't just for you, you know," Fitch said, feeling a lump in his throat, patting her arm, looking over her shoulder at the road ahead. "I did it for the guy in the mirror too. A thing like that, you walk away from it and it damned well eats you." And he was thinking about his cancer.

"The stuff of superheroes." She hugged him again, didn't matter he was driving.

"Nothing like that."

"But you weren't scared, right?"

"Wasn't time for it."

"And you knew he was coming, right?"

"I had a hunch."

"You know you swore again."

"Was hoping you missed it."

"Nope."

"Better get that jar."

She tapped her temple. "Keeping track up here. You're nearly at five bucks."

"Well, guess I'm no stranger to debt." And he was thinking of the chemo, and maybe hanging around a little longer. Sure Annie wouldn't mind waiting.

"You worried about it, aren't you, about money?"

"You ask a lot of questions for a kid."

"Are you?"

He looked at her. Man, this kid was sharp. "Maybe a little, but nothing you need to worry about. Hey, how about you just be a kid for a while."

"Meaning we'll get by."

"Sure we will." Fitch liked the sound of "we."

"And like I told you before, I'm chipping in," she said, and held up her hand to stop him from answering back. Then she reached behind her seat and pulled out the Canucks bag, unzipping it so he could see inside. Smiling, knowing he was about to swear again.

Acknowledgments

It has been a pleasure working with my publisher, Jack David, and the team at ECW Press over the years. I am grateful for their support, and I appreciate the excellence and care they bring to every novel. Many thanks to Emily Schultz, who is a talented and motivating force. I am truly fortunate to have her as my editor. Additionally, I thank my copyeditor, Peter Norman, for his outstanding attention to detail, and Michel Vrana for his creativity on the cover design.

A special thanks to my cousin, Charlotte Kenning, for cheering me on and for her medical expertise, which was a big help with this book.

As always, I am most grateful to my family, Andrea and Xander, for their love and inspiration.